The Dalton Family Adventures

Robert O. French

ISBN: 978-1-4669-4115-1 (sc)
ISBN: 978-1-4669-4116-8 (e)

Trafford rev. 06/01/2012

 www.trafford.com

North America & international
toll-free: 1 888 232 4444 (USA & Canada)
phone: 250 383 6864 ♦ fax: 812 355 4082

Contents

PART 1
Marshals, Miners, Merchants, Ministers, and Outlaws

PART 2
The Daltons: Lawmen In-Laws and Outlaws

PART 3
Blood Brothers "Life-Long Friends"

Acknowledgment

Randall "Randy" Michael Dalton
Consultant—Historical investigation and research

It is with grateful appreciation to Randy Dalton and Ray Stevens that this work has been completed due to a chance meeting on the high plains of the Colorado Rocky Mountains at a Men's Retreat. The encapsulated version of this story was shared with Randy and Ray without the knowledge that Randy's last name was Dalton. Randy later informed me that he is related to the members of the original family who made up the notorious Dalton Gang also referred to as the "Wild Bunch."

A special thanks to Ray and Randy for their encouragement, support, and interest. My promise to them was this work of fiction would become a reality. During the time we spent at the Men's Retreat, Randy shared some of his life experiences. I asked him if he would share these stories with us and he has graciously agreed.

A Pound of Hamburger

It was the winter if 1981. My wife, Linda, and I had just gotten back together after about a 6-month separation. We had lost just about everything due to the collapse of the economy in 1979. Interest rates skyrocketed to over 21 percent. What had been a dream come true with our new business started and opened to the public in the summer of 1975 suddenly turned to a nightmare almost overnight. The loss of income, the large debt, the uncertainty of our ability to recover from the loss, and the pressure were just too much for Linda. She had decided to leave our home. I was staring at a mountain of debt I had no way of paying.

Six months later, I had a life changing experience. I had received Jesus Christ as my Lord and Savior—I was "Born Again." I had a new job at a Christian radio station. I had worked there for a few months when I was fired for giving my opinion and for questioning the General Manager about his less-than-Christian conduct with a female employee. I was driving home wondering how I was going to explain to my wife, with whom I was newly reconciled, why I was fired from my job.

While driving home, I received a message on my pager with the number from a phone counselor from the 700 Club. I pulled over and called her back just to see why I was being contacted. I was in no real hurry to get home on a Thursday in the early afternoon just to explain why I was home so early in the day. The phone counselor was trying to assist a young family (of seven) find a place to stay for a short term. They had just lost everything due to a fire in the northeast section of Kansas City. It just happened the house we were living in had a full functioning two-bedroom apartment in the basement. Without another thought, I told the counselor, my wife and I would allow this family to stay in our basement apartment. (I had not asked my wife if this would be ok.) I have always told people I was full of faith. In making this decree, my family and the general public thought "I was full of something else." As for me, I am staying with "<u>full of faith</u>."

I want to set the stage for what happened next. Yes, the air was thick with tension. I would be lying if I said I was more than just a little concerned about my decision, not for making the decision, but for not consulting my wife prior to offering our basement apartment to the needy family. I was very concerned with one question, "What would be my wife's response?" But, I did feel amazingly sure I had done the right thing. Linda, on the other hand, I later found out, was not as convinced as I was. I picked up the family of seven in my Ford Econ-o-line van and brought them to our home. It was about 3:30 p.m. by this time. In a short time after some initial hasty explanations, our house guests were settled in the basement. I then asked Linda to see what we could do about dinner. So here we are, two-plus families. I say plus because I forgot to mention we were already foster parents of a 14-year-old girl who was pregnant in her third month. Our family count was three boys (Michael, Brett, Richard), Linda, and me.

So let's do a quick count and see just how many we have. There's me, my wife, our three boys, foster daughter, and a family of seven in the basement. Ok, I need both hands and one of my feet, no, I had better include one of Linda's hands. I count 13—we all know that, right? I had just walked to the kitchen and looked through the door, when I saw Linda standing at the counter, tears were falling to the floor. I was overcome with her pain. I instantly realized; I might have gone too far. I backed away from the door; and said a prayer, "God, I know you love us and would not let us down, now thank you, in Jesus name, Amen."

I stepped back through the door and put my arms around my wife's shoulders and told her how much I loved her. She spoke to me through quivering lips, "There is only a pound of hamburger here—this is not enough to feed us, let alone seven more people." I took a deep breath, "Linda, you do what you can, and God will do the rest." One hour later we all sat down at the table, thanked God for all he had done for us, and started eating. We all ate, our guests in the basement ate. They had nothing to eat for over 24 hours prior due to the tragedy they had experienced the day before. My boys ate and ate, because that's what they did every day. Our foster daughter ate and ate because she was eating for two. Linda ate a little bit because she wanted to make sure everyone had something to eat. I ate and ate because, I was pretty sure Linda was going to beat me up again for doing all of this to her.

But here's the deal; this is what happened. God's Word will do what God said it would do. Ask and believe, nothing is too hard for him. Not only did we all eat, there were burgers left over, glory be to God. "Ask and it shall be given you; seek, and ye shall find; knock, and it shall be opened unto you; for everyone that asketh receiveth; and he that seeketh findeth; and to him that knocks it shall be opened." Matthew 7:7-8. "O, Thou God who hearest prayer," Psalms 65:2 a. "Put it in our hearts to believe thee, and to pray."

Twelve Years to the Day

I can't remember a time that I have felt such despair, misery, and inner pain. My family—Linda my wife and three sons—meant everything to me. I thought, I was the luckiest man on the planet between the fall of 1979 until sometime in 1980, when the proverbial poo hit the fan. In my world, it had not let up, not even a little bit. Every day was another blow somewhere at any time. I think I felt like Sylvester Stallone looked in the movie "Rocky."

Well, it finally happened. Linda just couldn't take it anymore; and she took the boys and left. That happened in the summer of 1981. We had been arguing and yelling at each other for quite a while, and eventually she had enough. Suffice it to say, neither of us handled things very well at that time, as I now recall. Everything around us was out of control, so we were out of control. I was utterly alone; almost everything I had owned was gone, now my family was gone as well. I spoke from a broken heart, doubt, and unbelief in what had happened, "Good job, Randy. How's everything working out for ya??"

Let me give you the time line, starting within the next week.

I was now on the verge of a complete mental and emotional breakdown. I decided to go to a health clinic specializing in mental health problems, including but not limited to anxiety, depression, and suicide. Upon entering, I was seeking mental and emotional help. I was in the worst mental shape of my entire existence. I was asked for my insurance card. I said, "I don't have insurance due to losing every worldly possession when I previously lost my business." They couldn't help me (unbelievable, but true). I decided to make my way to my Mom and Dad's home, a place where I could possibly put things together for myself. I talked with them, but they really didn't know what to say or give me any advice about what I should do. My dad finally decided to give me $20 and said, "Here, son, take this money go buy a bottle of booze and get drunk."

I decided to get in my car and drive, I didn't know where. After about 20 minutes, I was sitting at a stoplight. I noticed off to my left was a Christian Book Store. I pulled in, I had a notion, a feeling inside, to take the $20 my father had given me and buy my first Bible. So instead of booze, I bought a Bible. I started feeling like things were starting to fall into place. I got back in the car with my newly purchased Bible. A thought came into my mind, "I need to go and talk to Dan's parents." Dan and I had been close friends for many years. "Why?" you might ask. Dan's parents know about God. They could show me in my new Bible where to find the help I needed.

Melvin and Ruth were two of the most loving and gentle souls I have ever met. They saw the shape I was in, and they knew what to do. They listened to me, just listened. But then they did something I had never experienced before. They prayed for me. Not just a little prayer, but a get in the devil's face—a very serious no messing around kind of prayer. A no B.S. kind of prayer. Now don't be alarmed, I wasn't saved yet. This is how I perceived things at the time. They were kicking tail and taking names. WOW! Something happened when they were finished. I really felt better. I had no fear. I was not anxious about anything. Then they asked me if I wanted to know Jesus, and if I wanted the love of God to come into my life. I said, "Yes." They prayed, and I prayed and received Jesus Christ as my Lord and Savior.

The next day was Sunday, and they asked me to join them at church. I don't remember even setting down before tears started running down my cheeks. I couldn't stop them. I had never felt such love like this before. The next thing I knew, I had my arms in the air and I was praising the Lord. Then out of my mouth come a bunch of words I did not understand, nor could I stop the words I was speaking out of my mouth. People around me were all doing the same thing. Some of them were falling down and lying on the floor; they were still saying whatever it was they were saying and they still had their arms raised.

On Saturday I was saved, and Sunday morning I was filled with the Holy Ghost! Yeah, things were turning around. I had to tell you about getting filled with the Holy Ghost so I can tell you what else I really want to say. My wife was still gone, and when we talked she reminded me often as to her feelings toward me. This part of my story was really quite difficult. I was going through a very hard time in my life. I was still struggling with mental and emotional anxiety being separated from my family, and Linda filed for divorce. Linda said, "I am not changing my mind, it's over—Get It!!!

Days, weeks, and months slowly passed. I had been reading God's Word every day. I had learned to speak the Word. I now understand what it means to stand on his promises. I learned many biblical truths that are essential to spiritual growth. I prayed, fasted, stood on the word, and spoke God's word over every situation in my life. I grew in faith and practice.

I was at the place in my life where I had grown in the Word. I knew God loves me. I know he wants me to have the desires of my heart. I know God hates divorce. I was, on one hand, riding the fence with my faith. I spoke and prayed one thing. My head told me another thing I didn't want to hear. So, I panicked just a little, right? No, no, I panicked a lot. So here I went. I will by God's grace see things my way. What I mean is, I am saved, I am born again, a child of the Most High God. My wife Linda, the mother of our children, is not. She needs to be.

I finally decided to go to God in prayer. He loves me and he wants what's best for me, right? So, I decided to go to my Father and beg like a little kid. WARNING! Watch what comes out of your mouth. I prayed, "Oh, Father God, Thank you for answering my prayers. Thank you for bringing my family back to me. Thank you, thank you, thank you. If I can just have 12 more years of my marriage, so my boys don't have to grow up in a broken home. Oh, thank you, Lord, so much for all you do and have done. In Jesus mighty name, Amen."

That prayer was spoken aloud in the summer of 1982. In a short time, one miracle happened after another and my broken marriage was restored. Just the day before my soon to be ex-wife had told me there was no way to save our marriage. But, I had prayed and I asked that my family come back to me. Where there was no way, God made a way. Through a minor fender bender on a well traveled six-lane street, my wife was thrown out of the car and hit her head. The police responded, an ambulance came, and Linda was taken to the hospital. This all happened only 6 blocks from her parents' home. Linda could not think of anyone else to call but me. The only number she could give to the police officer was mine, my telephone number at home. It was in the middle of the afternoon in the middle of the week. I just happened to be home at that exact time to take the call. I went to the hospital, and they released her and we went home. We were together from that point on, happier than we had ever been. The divorce was gone, just like that. My family was all back together like we were never apart.

Fast forward. It is now the summer of 1994, and I can see Linda is a little tired, run down a bit. So I said, "Sweetheart, no cooking tonight. Let's go get something to eat." On the drive to our favorite Chinese restaurant, Linda was quieter than usual. I knew she was tired. We had given the waitress our order, and we were sitting waiting for our food. I was about to take my first sip of ice tea when Linda looked up at me and said, "I filed for divorce today." I just sat there staring. I couldn't believe what I had just heard her say.

It was almost 12 years to the day since I had prayed my prayer asking for 12 years. That was what I received—exactly what I had asked. That evening sitting, staring in deep thought, I was stunned to find myself in similar circumstances that I had been in years before. I couldn't believe what I had heard. I was genuinely surprised and taken off guard. I never saw any indication or warning signs of this happening until Linda said "I filed for divorce today." I haven't returned to that restaurant since that day. After all these years, just driving by brings up those old memories of that difficult time.

Twelve years later I found myself going through a very rough time again. I just lost it all over again. I thought, "I know what is happening. God has done this to me." That night I was in my backyard at about midnight, screaming, cussing, and telling God just what I thought about him and his ways, as I was again reminding him about what had happened to my marriage.

Then I heard a voice speak to me. "Randy, my dear son, that is what you asked for, you decreed that."

Without hesitation, I dropped to my knees. I knew my loving Heavenly Father was right. I am his son. I am his child. I had asked for that very thing. I asked and believed with all that was within me. I had decreed a thing. The words that I had spoken aloud came into being. God did not do that. I said it, I did it, I decreed this very thing with my own words out of my own mouth.

"Through the death, burial, and resurrection of the Lord Jesus Christ," God gave us the same power to use here on earth that he himself used to speak into existence the universe. It is now 2011. What I just shared with you happened over 17 years ago. I still remember everything that happened—the prayer I prayed when I decreed a thing and especially the lessons I have learned from what was said, what I created with the words of my mouth.

Some related Bible verses for consideration are:

"But if the Spirit of him that raised up Jesus from the dead dwell in you, he that raised up Christ from the dead shall also quicken your mortal bodies by his Spirit that dwelleth in you." Romans 8:11

"Thou shalt also decree a thing, and it shall be established unto thee." Job 22:28

"Death and life are in the power of the tongue." Proverbs18:21

"What things soever ye desire, when ye pray, believe that ye receive them, and ye shall have them." Mark 11:24

"Let us make man in our image, after our likeness; and let them have dominion over the fish of the sea, and over the foul of the air, and over the cattle, and over all the earth, and over every creeping thing that creepeth upon the earth." Genesis 1:26

All verses above are from the King James Version.

The final reference is Psalms 45:1. (The New International Version gives the best translation.) "My heart is stirred by a noble theme as I recite my verse for the King; my tongue is the pen of a skillful writer."

Introduction

Jon James Robert Dalton—
Franklin Randall Dalton

Through their growing up years, both boys Frank and Jon spent time with their extended family members. Any given Sunday and every summer was spent with family which established devoted relationships with their relatives. Family reunions were not held every year, but they were usually 3- or 4-day weekends; and every Dalton looked forward to that time to visit and spend time with their extended family.

Frank Dalton met Abraham Lincoln in the spring of 1862 when he was 17 years old on a business trip with his father to Washington, D.C. Frank and his father were included in a group of guests to the White House for a brief meeting with the President of the United States. The visit was an informal meeting arranged by a Lincoln family member for some of his close friends. A question was asked about Abe's father whose name was Thomas Lincoln. Without hesitation, Abe mentioned his grandfather was also named Abraham. His great grandfather was called John—Tennessee John. The meeting was very special to Frank. It was a highlight in his life, for as much as he had lived by the age of 17.

Franklin Randall (Randy) Dalton, cousin of Jon, was 5 years older. Frank was born February 26, 1845, in Lamar, Missouri. He died December 2, 1936, at the age of 91.

Jon James Robert Dalton was born October 23, 1850, in Lamar, Missouri. He died October 25, 1950, at the age of 100 years and 2 days. The obituary mentioned he outlived two wives, and was survived by many children, grandchildren, and great grandchildren. He died of old age and was in excellent health until his demise. Jon Dalton wrote this poem at age 15 years, south of the Dalton home place in Lamar, Missouri.

"Life is not always fair nor is it just. God in his infinite mercy is Just."

The Lord looks down upon me from his throne on high.
I a mere man upon this rock I lay.
Every step I take, everywhere I stand.
My Master has come before me and will be once again.
His hand is on my shoulder; His image is in my heart.
The Lord Jesus is always with me, every task I start.
Jon James Robert Dalton

Part 1

Marshals, Miners, Merchants, Ministers, and Outlaws

Chapter One

Frank Dalton ventured out to Colorado lured by gold and untold fortune in the Colorado Rocky Mountains. The specific town of interest was originally Central City, Colorado. However, by chance, or fate might be a better word, the town of residence for Frank was the small and lesser-known town of Black Hawk, Colorado. It was just a short walk, a 1 mile hike down the canyon, from Central City.

Frank panned many of the creeks in the area that first year. Panning for gold was a very physically demanding art. The kneeling position required to do it caused muscle pain in the back, arms, and legs and would after a short while demand standing up.

In the afternoons after a particularly successful day, Frank quit early and walked to the Gilpin Hotel in Black Hawk. During the last 2 weeks, he had spent some of the summer nights sleeping out on the ground. Usually the colder nights were spent in a cabin up the canyon half way between Central City and Black Hawk. Three other men owned the cabin and room was made on the floor for a night inside away from the cold. Frank met the men shortly after his arrival.

Frank was walking down the canyon from the north past the smelter stamping mill. The long dark copper-colored buildings of the operation made the largest one structure in the area. He had panned for 2 weeks and today He carried the results of his panning of gold dust in his pack. He had panned from his favorite areas, and it had been a great 2 weeks. Frank was tired and walked slowly into the smelter assay office and cashed in his dust. "Not bad, not bad at all," said the assayer.

Frank folded the bills and pushed them into the front pocket of his pants, tipped his hat to the assayer, and walked out. He was now smiling as he walked and visualized his final destination: 111 Main Street, the Gilpin Hotel.

The Gilpin Hotel was where occasionally he would treat himself to a good meal, a bath, and a good night's sleep in a real bed. That was very rare; but a good meal with a few great cups of coffee was always a fitting reward for 2 weeks of work well done. He was at the east end of the smelter which was parallel to the Main Street of the town. Gregory Street was the first street of the town, which was the street that went all the way up to Central City. It was named after the man who was responsible for the original discovery of gold in the area.

He walked up Gregory Street until he was parallel with Main Street in Black Hawk. He then walked east across the street to 101 Main Street. Frank had been watching a man walk slowly down Gregory Street past Crooks Saloon, one of the first saloons open for business in the area. They had a sign in the window proclaiming, "The First." They had good food, but it was occasionally frequented with the wild and unruly sort, and Frank was craving some peace and quiet.

The man stopped on the opposite corner from Frank and was standing looking down the street.

You never knew who anyone was just from his or her appearance or where anyone might be traveling. The hat he wore and his clothes were of a style Frank had seen in a Kansas City store window, although now they looked dirty, soiled, and dusty. The man looked very tired, completely physically spent, as if he needed to rest before he took another step.

Frank walked up and introduced himself extending his hand to greet the man. The man smiled, took Frank's hand, then started moving his face up and down slowly as he moved his hand in the same up and down rhythm. "Howard French, Kansas City, Kansas." he said.

"Pleasure to meet you," said Frank. "I live about 120 miles south of Kansas City, Missouri. It's a small town called Lamar, Missouri."

Frank still slowly shaking the man's hand said, "I am going down to the Gilpin Hotel, there on the right, to have a cup of coffee and a good meal. You are welcome to join me. In fact, sir, I insist! The meal is on me."

"No, no, I don't expect that. I am a stranger—you don't owe me a thing."

"Well, the Good Lord says to share and help those who may be in need. With all due respect, sir, you look like you could use a good meal. I would really enjoy the company—allow me," said Frank. "Will you join me for a good meal?" When Frank released the man's hand, it fell slowly to his side.

With a wide smile Frank said, "I have a relative named Dan French who says, "We shouldn't eat alone if we can possibly help it. Dan has a brother named Jim who I am sure would also agree. It's good to have company during a meal, allowing for good conversation."

"Well, thank you, young man. I will join you. I could certainly use a cup of coffee and a good meal. I am feeling right famished," said Howard, with a half smile and nod of his head. He had a smile and a way about him that made you feel good to be around him.

Chapter Two

Frank led the way as the two men entered the hotel lobby and walked to the dining room where the waitress recognized Frank. Smiling at her, Frank said, "Two cups of coffee to get us started."

As the two men sat down, Frank said, "This dining area is usually reserved for the hotel guests. I occasionally check in and spend the night. On second thought, I am sure if paying customers with gold dust came into the hotel, the management would not refuse service to any paying customer."

"I would guess you are a prospector looking for a rich area where you can stake your claim. I am rambling on," said Frank, "Excuse me for dominating the conversation. I decided to eat here at the hotel today as it is like a treat to myself for an exceptionally good week of panning."

The man removed his hat, exposing a dark bruise on his forehead which looked like it could use medical attention.

"Looks like you have hit your head. You need a doctor to look at that," said Frank.

"I fell this morning while I was hiking north of Central City. It is a lot better than it was right after I fell. I had a hard time seeing at first. I completed my work for Phillips Mining in Central City. I then decided I wanted to look at some of the area for myself before returning to Kansas City."

"I am a Mining Engineer. I was hiking and collecting ore samples. I was interested in some rock outcropping. I was making a loop around through the mining encampment just north and west of Central City—Nevadaville, I think it's called," Howard said.

"You say you had trouble seeing right after you hit your head?" asked Frank.

"Yeah, I did. I could have passed out from the fall. I think I must have just sat there for a while. The pain hurt something awful for the longest time. I still have a dull headache," said Howard.

Frank asked the waitress if she knew where the Doc might happen to be.

"I think he's upstairs playing poker," she said.

"Take a cup of coffee up to the Doc, and tell him it's on me, Frank Dalton. Tell him I have a friend that's . . ."

The young waitress smiled, "I heard what your friend said and what happened to him. I'll be right back with the Doc. I'll not be taking him any coffee. If I take him coffee, he will stay up there and drink it."

Frank had poured his coffee in the small saucer holding the cup and was blowing across the hot liquid while he occasionally sipped it. "This process is called saucer blowing."

The Doc arrived shortly after the waitress had disappeared upstairs. Seeing him enter the dining room, Frank stood up and said, "Sorry, Doc, about getting you out of the poker game."

"No matter, I wasn't winning any way. What do we have here?" asked Doc, as he sat his bag on the empty chair across from Frank. He sat down in the last remaining chair at the table. He extended his hand and said, "My name's Doc Towne, Gordon Towne, Gordon or Doc to my friends."

Frank's dinner guest introduced himself, "I am" hesitating slightly, "I am Howard H. French. I am a Mining Engineer and work for Phillips Mining & Engineering out of Kansas City, Kansas. We sell and maintain smelting and mining equipment. We specialize in stamping mills and maintain the parts and offer service and repair. We sell to most of the mills locally—Idaho Springs, Central City, and Black Hawk."

"A professional college educated degreed man—I like that," said Doc. "You do have a nasty bruise on your forehead. How did that happen?"

"I fell while I was looking for ore samples earlier this morning or maybe it was yesterday. It all seems a little cloudy to me," said Howard.

"Well, you mind if I take a look at that, dress it, tend to it for you? Come with me," said Doc. He stood, picked up his satchel, and started to exit with his new patient following close behind.

Doc looked at the waitress, "Jenny, I need a cup of coffee." Holding his hand out toward her, the thumb and forefinger about an inch apart. "About that much of the 12-year-old Scotch in it, OK?" With a quick wink at Jenny and a nod as he looked at Frank, Doc said. "We'll be right back, I have a room upstairs. I will join you gentlemen for dinner, if that would be all right with you, Frank?"

"My treat," said Frank smiling. In an instant, he was back to his saucer blowing and coffee sipping.

Doc and Howard returned a while later. After the three gave the waitress their order, Doc said to Frank, "I believe Howard was knocked unconscious when he hit his head a day or a couple of days ago. I told him no charge for the medical care due to the supper you offered, Frank. But he insisted on paying, saying he had money. As he looked through his pack, he discovered the ore samples and the cash missing. Someone must have come upon him while he was unconscious and took his money and all the ore samples he had collected. He doesn't remember walking through Central City. He surely walked that way to end up here at the Gilpin Hotel."

"We just met outside at the corner of Gregory and Main here in Black Hawk," said Frank.

Doc answered, "He does remember meeting you and your supper invitation. He might be suffering from a mild case of amnesia. Total amnesia will take most if not all the memory and he wouldn't know who he is. I recommend a few days' bed rest and observation. But I need to go about making my rounds of the mining camps. I have a schedule, and am expected tomorrow in Central City. I am not available to stay here in Black Hawk and keep an eye on him, not right now anyway.

Frank excused himself from the table and returned just before the food arrived. "I have a room key here for the two of us. I explained the situation to the Hotel Manager and owner. Howard can sleep in the bed, and I'll sleep on the couch and keep an eye on him. We have a single rate for 3 days."

"That's perfect," said Doc, "I feel far better about this situation. I'll be back by then and check on Howard. I'll make a decision when I examine him in 3 days. I would think a full week of bed rest might be necessary to determine if he has any lasting damage. Only time will tell."

"I could go to any of the mills my company does business with, and they would cash a voucher or cash a check from my company. Phillips Mining Equipment in Kansas City could verify and release funds for expenses through any of the mills. We have accounts with some of the largest mills," said Howard.

"I rarely if ever have to do such a thing; but in light of the fact I was robbed, I am sure it wouldn't be a problem. I could wire my company from Denver. They would release funds to one of the local banks for any travel expenses I might have."

"That's not necessary, Howard," said Frank. "The Bible tells a story how a man was beaten, robbed, and left for dead. Another man came along and found him, treated his wounds, and took him to an inn or a hotel—it was called an inn in the Bible. The Good Samaritan treated his wounds and paid the inn keeper money for the man to stay in a room in the inn until he had recovered. Your story is not exactly like the one in the Bible, but it's similar. Howard, allow me to be a Good Samaritan. In the future down the road, you will have the opportunity to help someone in need. It's the Golden Rule. Luke 6:31, 'And as ye would that men should do to you, do ye also to them likewise.' Do unto others as you would want others to do unto you. It's the Golden Rule, simple as pie."

"Doc says you need bed rest for at least 3 days—maybe longer. You are not in any shape to take the stage from Black Hawk back to Denver. Is he, Doc?" asked Frank.

"No, not at all, I wouldn't recommend it," responded Doc. "Howard, I suggest you listen to the young man. The stage ride alone would cause physical stress, which is the last thing you need now. You need at least 3 days—maybe more—to let your body heal from this concussion. What else do you have to do? Man, you could have died up there unconscious on that mountain," said Doc shaking his head with a firm look on his face.

"Frank, you don't need to stay in the room every minute. Go get the man some more ore samples for his office back in Kansas City. Have Jenny look in on him a few times during the day while you are out. She will need to take his lunch to the room. You can pan for gold and do whatever. It's the night and early morning I want you near him. Just watch for unusual behavior—slurred speech, stiffness in areas of his body, anything out of the ordinary. I really don't expect any symptoms like that this long after the incident," said Doc.

"Gentlemen, let's eat. This food is getting cold," said Doc. "I am sure you two old miners will have many stories to swap. The next 3 days, you two will be forced to eat three squares here at the hotel. That shouldn't be hard to take. Some scenery always looks good every time you look. That waitress, Jenny—she certainly adds to the scenery here in this dining room," said Doc with a low cackle sounding laugh.

Turning in his chair after seeing her reflection in the window, Doc said, "Jenny, another cup of coffee, and holding his thumb and forefinger about an inch apart, One more of, you know, about that much, 12-year-old Scotch." Nodding his head and smiling he said, "Thanks, you are a sweetheart."

As Jenny walked away, Doc was staring at the shapely young lady walking into the kitchen. "I think that girl needs her yearly physical," he said quietly to himself almost under his breath. Then he said in a louder tone, "She has assisted me with a number of patients. She has real natural ability. She makes a great nursing assistant, and is a quick learner. You need to marry that girl, Frank. You couldn't do better."

Doc leaned forward and said, "I could have been a miner digging in the dirt and panning for gold in freezing water, until my legs were asleep, my hands aching from arthritis pain. But no, I became a doctor." Looking over his glasses at both men, he started to laugh when he said, "Those prospectors out in those hills only have gold dust to pay me for my services. Damn, I am still doing ok, even if I say so myself." He then filled his mouth with mashed potatoes and smiled as he slowly chewed his first bite of some of the best food served in Black Hawk. He looked out the window of the Hotel as he continued to eat with a look on his face as if he were thinking of a different place and a different time.

The next 3 days were filled with more than enough time for Howard to rest, recover, and regain strength from the stress his body had experienced. He shared all he felt Frank should know for the type of prospecting and mining he would eventually need to do to fulfill his dreams. Howard gave Frank another gift that Frank would not realize until he applied the principles to his life. He shared all he could about the laws and principles of life. He gave Frank a five-page letter, all neatly handwritten on Gilpin Hotel stationary.

The letter expressed great thanks for his kindness and a promise of future communication. From the gracious "Thank you" on page one to the signature on page five, "To Frank Dalton my protégé."

Howard made Frank his protégé because of his desire to teach and train a younger man about the laws of life.

Chapter Three

THE GILPIN HOTEL
111 MAIN SREET—BLACK HAWK, COLORADO

Page 1

Mr. Franklin Randall Dalton:

I want to express my heartfelt gratitude to you for your work as a Good Samaritan. You confessed you are a child of God doing the work of your Lord Jesus. Few to none have openly helped me in a time of dire need as you have. I extend to you my appreciation and desire for you to visit my home in Independence, Missouri. I would gladly introduce you to my family, insist you be my guest at my favorite restaurant, and visit some of the great sites of my city. Doing this in return for your unselfish kindness so graciously expressed to me.

I will share a quote from Ralph Waldo Emerson's book. "The secret is the answer to all that has been, all that is, and all that will ever be." A secret? The secret mentioned here could be the "Rule of Attraction." The secret of success is attracted to you by the images you hold in your mind, what you are thinking or picturing in your mind as you go to sleep. We have laws in this world all around us. The law of gravity always works if you are a good or a bad person—if you fall from a tree, you will hit the ground. The laws of this earth work every time, all the time, as the Father God, Jesus Christ the creator designed all things to work together in harmony. Read the books of Genesis and John to better understand God's creation and God's plan of redemption and salvation of man.

A magnet works with specific laws. I see myself as a magnet. I attract positive things.

Our thoughts have presence and create feelings that flow out of us all the time.

Good thoughts, good things visualized, and good words sent out will attract positive results to your life and will eventually manifest your words from the spirit into the natural real world.

You become what you think about and attract what you think about. What is visualized in your mind, you will eventually hold in your hand. Thoughts have a frequency—every thought, good and bad, has a specific frequency. I am a living soul. I determine how I think and speak. Both project a frequency to people and to life all around us.

I Chronicles 28:9b, "For the Lord searches every heart and understands every motive behind the thoughts. If you seek him, he will be found by you; but if you forsake him, he will reject you forever."

This scripture is in reference to the thoughts of a man, do you understand? Let's stop here and ask a question. According to the Bible, God created the Universe—all we see, feel, and touch. Let's try to describe God: always was, always has been; never can be created or destroyed; all there ever was, all there ever will be; always moving into form, through form, and out of form. Read the book of John. This will reveal the Gospel and God's plan for the redemption of all mankind.

THE GILPIN HOTEL
111 MAIN SREET—BLACK HAWK, COLORADO

Page 2

It is God's nature to hear and answer prayer. "O thou that hearest prayer, unto thee shall all flesh come." Psalms 65:2 It is impossible to come to God or to please him without believing that he is a prayer-hearing and a prayer-answering God. "But without faith it is impossible to please him; for he that cometh to God must believe that he is, and that he is a rewarder of them that diligently seek him." Hebrews 11:6 Every attribute of God is implied in the fact that he hears and answers prayers.

Attributes are qualities and characteristics of God implied when we believe God is a prayer-hearing God and he answers the prayer of his children. When the priests of Baal on Mount Carmel cried out to their God, "O, Baal, hear us," there was no answer. I Kings 18:26, Then God's prophet, Elijah, prayed and the prayer-hearing God answered and did all that was asked.

God didn't command his children to sing without ceasing or to work without ceasing. No. He did say, "Pray without ceasing." I Thessalonians 5:17 It would appear prayer and praying often is necessary and beneficial. In the Book of Acts, the apostles in the early church selected deacons to do the work of caring for the widows and the poor. This gave the apostles the time needed to pray—again signifying the importance of prayer. Please read and consider Acts 6:4, "But we will give ourselves continually to prayer, and the ministry of the word."

Don't get impatient; just keep praying and seek the Lord for the answers. The answers will come, it must, it will come to pass. When bad or negative thoughts come into your mind, DO NOT dwell or think about them. These thoughts might not be your thoughts in the first place. Read II Corinthians 10:5b, "bringing into captivity every thought to the obedience of Christ."

Once you see how to master your own thought life and feelings, that is when you will see how to truly pray and confess who and what you are in Christ Jesus. Don't get impatient—this has been a detriment to the success of many men. When you are focused and deliberate in your positive thought life, you will become the man living the life you now visualize for yourself and with confession you will become. Say aloud: "Therefore if any man be in Christ, he is a new creature: old things are passed away; behold, all things are become new." II Corinthians 5:17 "I am a child of God, I am born again."

To review: Thoughts have a frequency. Think a thought, in your mind see it, visualize it, picture it in your mind. See yourself already having what you are praying for, living in wealth and abundance, and you will attract it. Negative people are visualizing and thinking about what they don't want, what they fear might happen. They say aloud: "We have no hope with so much debt." "I have so many health problems." "I will never see my bills paid off." "My problems will never go away." If this thinking is your thinking, if these words are your words, stop it right now. Thoughts of failure bring failure.

THE GILPIN HOTEL
111 MAIN SREET—BLACK HAWK, COLORADO

Page 3

The negative thinking person eventually attracts the sum total of his or her thoughts and will always wonder why life's woes come over and over again. The subconscious mind all humans have works as an obedient slave. The subconscious mind doesn't care if you perceive something to be good or bad, if you want it or not. The subconscious mind responds to your most persistent thoughts. The law of words and the law of attraction are always working. Read Matthew 15:18: "But the things that come out of the mouth, come from the heart, and these make a man unclean."

Frank, you told me you are a child of God, that you received Jesus Christ as your Lord and Savior. Frank, spiritually speaking, you are born of God. You have God's nature. The life of God dwells with you. You are his child. He is your Father. Say this confession aloud: "I am a new creature in Christ Jesus. I am a child of the most high God. I am a joint heir with Jesus Christ. I am the righteousness of God in Christ Jesus."

"Nay, in all these things we are more than conquerors through him that loved us." Frank Dalton is more than a conqueror through him that loved us. Read aloud Romans 8:37.

What does the word of God say in Psalms 23:1? "The Lord is my shepherd; I shall not want." Read Psalm 34:10: "The young lions do lack, and suffer hunger, but they that seek the Lord shall not want any good thing." God says he will give us our wants. So speak aloud with your mouth what you want. Confess aloud a verbal prayer of each thing you want or need and believe it is already present in your life. Visualize what it is you want, and experience the feelings and emotions as if you already have them as a part of your life. Visualize in your mind, confess you have them, feel and act as if you possess them.

A man had a large debt that seemed impossible to ever pay. Using the law of confession after he built up his faith with the word of God and understood how it worked, he watched his debt disappear. Below is part of a letter he wrote to me.

Instruction: People who think incorrectly, believe incorrectly; and when they believe incorrectly, they are wrong. I searched the scriptures for God's promises, made a list, and confess them daily. Read Mark 11:23-24 to understand. First: Whosoever speaks to the mountain, says 'be removed,' does not doubt, and believes that those things he says will come to pass, he will have whatever he says. I took every bill and debt and placed them on the floor in my home. I said, "Bills and debts, listen to me. I am talking to you. Jesus said you would obey me. In the name of the Lord Jesus Christ, I command you, I say to you, 'BE PAID IN FULL—DEMATERIALIZE—DEPART—BE GONE.' In Jesus name, you will obey me." Don't say any negative words; guard your mouth until all you confessed happens. Be thankful, close your eyes, see yourself feeling the way you know you will feel with all debt paid in full. In reality, it is already paid in the spirit and will manifest in the natural. Signed, Mr. Debt Free, Sr.

THE GILPIN HOTEL
111 MAIN SREET—BLACK HAWK, COLORADO

Page 4

Our lives and our world are governed by laws. Consider the law of confession, Proverbs 18:20-21: "A man's belly shall be satisfied with the fruit of his mouth; and with the increase of his lips shall he be filled. Death and life are in the power of the tongue; and they that love it shall eat the fruits thereof." The law of words: speak it forth, say the word aloud. "So then faith comes by hearing, and hearing by the Word of God." Romans 10:17

The story goes that Aladdin takes the lamp and polishes, and rubs the lamp. The Jeanie appears and his comment is always the same: "Your wish is my command." The original story was told that there was no limit to the wishes. Think about that for a while. The life long application of the law of attraction and the law of words, speaking your future into existence. Guard your mouth, and make it a habit to not speak words that are in opposition to what you have confessed and believed to be coming into your life. My dear friend, it is up to you to practice and see how these laws work.

The police, law enforcement, Pinkerton men, the crime investigators say: "To catch a thief, you must think like a thief." They really don't completely understand why or how it works—they just know it does. Well, here is why. Think with the like frequency or vibration, and you start to attract who and what you are seeking. That is just my personal belief, but I believe it will prove to be true.

The criminal-minded negative thinker breaks the LAW, commits offense or crime, steals money, is eventually placed in prison because of fear, guilt, inherit desire for reconciliation to do the right thing if only on the subconscious level. They desire to make it right by visualizing options—the fear of being caught, arrested, placed in prison—and eventually they are. They are all drawn together to this place of recompense with society and with God. That place society calls jail, prison, or penitentiary where you pay for your crimes, do diligence, and repent. This force permeates the very soul of most human beings. In spite of the decision made to commit the crime in the first place, these people become their own worst enemy. Read in Job 3:25: "For the thing I greatly feared is come upon me, and that which I was afraid of is come unto me."

Stay away from negative thoughts and negative people. The Bible answer concerning your thoughts, "Take every thought captive." II Corinthians 10:5b. The unruly thoughts of a man can destroy him. "Death and Life are in the power of the tongue." Proverbs 18:21. Don't destroy what you have built with words spoken against what you desire. Guard your mouth from cursing what you desire. A friend in this life and a brother in eternity.

Signed: Howard Henry French, August 2, 1882

Robert O. French

THE GILPIN HOTEL
III MAIN SREET—BLACK HAWK COLORADO
Page 5

Frank Dalton:

I have some notable quotes I want to share with you. Perhaps one or more will inspire or motivate you as they have moved me on more than one occasion. Why do men do the things they do, and why are some so very driven to go above and beyond? I will again give you a gift another man gave me. But alas for now, I share some memorable quotes from people you might have never known except one. Author of the first quote is yours truly?

Some are content to never leave the security of home. Vagabonds and adventurers are in a league of their very own. But for each to determine to take that first step to pursue their dreams, few would never have started their journey. Howard Henry French

Without adventure, civilization is in full decline. Alfred North Whitehead

We are all travelers. In the wilderness of the world, and all the best we can find. In our travels is a human friend. Robert Louis Stevenson

However much you and all of us may desire it, there is not much hope of redemption without the shedding of blood. Henry Highland Garnet

All men dream, but not equally. Those who dream by night in the dusty recesses of their minds wake in the day to find that it was vanity; but the dreamers of the day are dangerous men, for they may act their dreams with open eye to make them possible. T.E. Lawrence, The Seven Pillars of Wisdom

I am myself plus my circumstances, and if I do not save it, I cannot save myself. Jose Ortega Y Gasso, "Meditations on Quixote"

The further one goes—The less one knows. Lao Tzu

It's not all pleasure, this exploration. David Livingstone April 19, 1873

I am dreaming of finding the lost city of Meroe, but reality reveals that I have lost nearly all my teeth. David Livingstone, Journals, 1873 Quotes from the book, "I met Livingstone" by Charles H. Stanley, New York Herald

If you're not living good, travel wide. Bob Marley

We proceeded on. LEWIS & CLARK, 1805

He who has not seen the Blue Nile will praise a stream. Ancient Ethiopian Proverb

If the primary aim of a captain were to preserve his ship, he would keep it in port forever. Thomas Aquinas

Fortune brings in some boats that are not steered. William Shakespeare

Mr. Frank Dalton, I wish you well and all the success to obtain the happiness you seek.

I am giving you a map and the instructions, all the information is written just exactly as it was given to me. The procedure for and the precise compliance to instructions are the payment for the wealth that will be yours if you desire to pursue it. The map and the instructions were given to me from a man of his word. I gave my word. You will be asked to do the same.

Signed: Howard Henry French, August 5, 1882

Chapter Four

Howard finally told Frank a story of a man he met the year before in Colorado Springs, Colorado.

Lou Spillman was visiting his brother who was in the hospital with a severe case of pneumonia. Howard was visiting a close friend, a doctor at the hospital. Lou was also a friend of the doctor. The doctor introduced Howard, a Mining Engineer, to Lou, an old time prospector who appeared from time to time to have struck it rich. Howard asked Lou if he could buy dinner, and he would be very interested in any and all Lou could tell him of what he had learned in his years of prospecting.

Lou suggested a good restaurant in the area. Howard asked if he could take notes, and he did, making notes and writing down much of what Lou told him. In short order, the men became friends and talked late into the night. The night being far spent, Lou said good night and left to go to his home, which was nearby.

The men had decided to have a late breakfast at the café near the hospital. They met the next morning and went to check on his brother. Howard prayed for the men and shared some verses from the small New Testament he carried in the pocket of his leather jacket. The Spillman brothers both prayed with Howard and were visibly changed. They both (Lou and Eddie) received the Lord Jesus Christ as Lord and Savior.

Howard was going to go to Pueblo, Colorado, and work with a company developing a coal mine in southern Colorado. He intended to stop back in Colorado Springs and come by the hospital to check on Eddie. The Spillman brothers were not at the hospital. The doctor gave Howard the address of their home.

Howard was aware from the greeting by Lou something serious had happened. The sad news of the loss of his brother, Eddie, had deeply affected Lou's mother. Her health was not that good before she heard of the loss of her son. She needed prayer, and Lou did not hesitate to ask Howard to pray for his mother.

Lou had the idea to have all his relatives come to his mother's house. Have Howard tell them all how Eddie and Lou were sure heaven would be their Heavenly Home. After the evening meal, the Spillman clan were all in the living room of Grandma's house. They all were hearing how Lou and Eddie were born again. It was true Eddie was gone from this world, but he was alive in heaven. He was alive forevermore. He had left this world, but they would see him in the future if they repented from their sins and became God's children.

Howard took the little New Testament and shared many scriptures of the simple plan of salvation with the complete family. He had them bow their heads and asked how many would like to receive the Lord Jesus Christ as their Lord and Savior. Every family member in the room raised their hand.

Howard said, "Lou and I will lead you in a simple prayer. Repeat after us a simple prayer of repentance and receive the Lord Jesus Christ as your Lord and Savior. Every family member prayed and received Jesus Christ as their Lord and Savior.

Grandma started laughing and said she had never been so happy. She took the hand of Lou's father, her husband for many years. She said, "I have loved you for almost all my life, and I will be with you forever for all eternity. You will be stuck with me and my love for you and the Lord Jesus Christ forever. My complete family—every one, heaven bound. This is a miracle, and it all happened in one day."

The local Baptist Church was 3 blocks away. They decided to walk down and see if the pastor lived nearby. The pastor lived just behind the church. He listened to what Howard and Lou shared and was pleased to add the Spillman family to his church. He had known of the hard drinking, wild living of the Spillman boys, especially Lou and Eddie. He was sorry to hear of Eddie passing away, but pleased to know heaven was his home. The funeral service could be scheduled at the church, and the hospital had already released the body to the local funeral home. The pastor knew the undertaker.

Lou asked, "What is the total cost for the undertaker, the church, and your services, Pastor?"

"The use of the church for the funeral and my services will all be at no charge for the Spillman family," said the Pastor smiling. "You need to check with the funeral home for the cost of the arrangements. Their services can be paid on a monthly basis. I can talk with them if you like," said the Pastor.

"Yes, please do," said Lou. "I will take my parents and my uncles, and we can set up all the arrangements."

The following Saturday would be an open date for the Pastor to schedule and conduct the funeral services. A Hallelujah service was what the Pastor said it would truly be. The families of the church would provide a potluck dinner, and the Spillman's would not need to bring any food. The church would take care of all potluck food arrangements.

"It's our honor to share with your family in this way in your hour of need. I will come with you now. We can walk to your home, and I will talk with your family," said the Pastor. "The Lord commands us to stand and make a profession of faith and follow the Lord Jesus in example and be baptized."

The meeting with the Pastor was perfect timing. It was decided the entire family would attend church on the Sunday after the funeral and all be baptized and accepted as members into the church.

Howard was aware of the quiet and somber way Lou was acting as they walked back to his home. "I think you mentioned you have some ore samples I could buy. The mining display in our office back in Kansas City is always in need of ore samples like you mentioned. I will almost bet you the amount will match whatever the undertaker fees are to the penny." Howard gave Lou another $100 for all the ore samples he had.

Lou said, "I really appreciate what you just did. This will keep me through the winter and stake me up to the mine in the spring. Thanks to you and the Lord Jesus, no more Mrs. Poker and Mr. Whiskey. You know that saying of the gambling hall: Liquor in the front and Poker in the rear."

Howard said, "Lou, that old saying is probably not the best to quote if you catch my meaning."

"You're right," said Lou smiling and nodding his head. Without a word of hesitation Lou said, "These ore samples are from a mine my brother and I found. We, my brother and I, have mined it for years. We have yet to even remove a tenth of the rich ore in that mine. The mountain is full of this high-grade ore. Me and Eddie decided if one of us died—well, he told me if he passed away to tell only one person about the mine. Telling only one person is our way of keeping this treasure from the world and the destruction of the land and the wealth of this area. I guess that's our decision to make. We prayed for the mountain and the precious ore that is buried will now be used for God's purpose whatever that might be."

"I believe Eddie would approve of revealing the location of the mine to a man like you, Howard. I will give you a map with the location with one stipulation. You never tell more than just one person of its exact geographical location. The world would swarm to this place, climb over the mountain, and spoil the wealth for everyone. That one person who you decide to tell must be of good character and personal trust—like a family member or close personal friend sealed with a handshake, giving your word to honor the original request. Like an oath of a witness in court sworn on a Bible. Mr. Howard French, do I have your word?" The men shook hands and spontaneously hugged each other.

"With Eddie gone, I am now the only one who knows the exact location of the mine. "Have you ever heard of Lost Park?" asked Lou. "Well, just past Lost Park is East Lost Park. Ever hear of that area? Well few have, and likely few ever will in consideration of finding gold. I hope that's always the way it will be. Do you have some paper? I will draw an exact map of the mine's location," said Lou. Within minutes, I was holding a folded paper in my hand.

"Frank, this paper is the only copy I have of the original map. I know I will never attempt to locate this mine. I never had any intention of trying to," said Howard. "You, Frank, are a man I would consider a friend and a brother in Christ. You have treated me well; I might as well consider you to be kin."

The paper Howard was holding was of a different type of paper. The drawing on the paper was a complete detailed map made by a man who must have been a surveyor or worked with a surveyor. The directions were concise and complete, easy to follow. "I sign and give this map to you, Frank Dalton, with the stipulation you must only tell one person. Signed: Howard Henry French, August 5, 1882. To Frank Dalton, the one I have chosen to tell of the location of the Spillman Mine. If you see a man on the mountain, in or near the mine, named Lou Spillman, show him this map—specifically my name and signature. Tell him you kept your word, just as I have kept my word. If a man or woman can't keep their word, what do you have? No honor and respect for their word given and kept. No honor, no code, no trust. If you give your word, a vow, keep your word and honor the vow."

"A man's word is his bond. I ask you to shake my hand. We will use this physical action as an act of agreement to seal what we have said between the two of us and God." Howard extended his hand and Frank gave a firm grasp. Looking into the eyes of Howard French, Frank said, "I give my word. I will do as you have said, and I will follow the instruction exactly as presented to you by Mr. Louis Spillman, so help me God."

"Your word is a vow to me and God," Howard said with a smile. The men hugged as if brothers, for brothers they were and had become. He said as he released Frank, "Thank you again for saving my life."

"Thank you, for sharing this gift," said Frank, his right hand touched the pocket in his shirt which held the map of a place he could now only imagine.

Howard said, "When I feel totally recovered from my fall, I am returning to Kansas City to my family and home. I have traveled far and wide for the company. I have worked for more years than I care to remember. I was planning on making some changes concerning the time away from my family. I need to just do more consulting, and let the younger fellows do the fieldwork. I don't believe I will ever use a map to travel south and search out this Spillman mine. You need to locate it and gain from the riches you find there. The proper mining of it could make you a wealthy man and you need to pray and ask God what he would have you do concerning the mine and the treasure of East Lost Park."

Howard took Frank's hand and said, "I would like to pray for you as you go and ask God's blessings on you and all you do from now on and the life you are seeking. Frank was moved to tears as the Holy Spirit ministered to him as Howard prayed. This was the last time Howard and Frank were together. Their lives went their separate ways—one east to home and family. Frank continued to do as he had before he met Howard French on the corner of Gregory and Main in Black Hawk, Colorado.

Chapter Five

In the spring of 1884 on May 30, it was time for Jon Dalton to move in the direction that he had been planning with his cousin Frank Dalton. To follow their dreams to travel out West for fame, fortune and adventure where ever that might lead them.

His father was an attorney and had practiced for many years before Jon was born. The work his father had developed was as an attorney, public prosecutor, trial lawyer, legal representative, notary for the banking business, and real estate investment. This was his father's vocation and had developed into a family business.

Jon read and studied from the twelfth through the seventeenth year of his life—a total of 5 years of his young life. Jon was to be the son who followed in his father's footsteps. He was a prodigy of his father and would eventually take over the firm and run the family business. Jon's father was a man of character and deep honorable principles.

Among the many things Jon learned from his father, the most important thing was every God-fearing person should become one of God's children when they receive Jesus Christ as Lord and Savior. Then the act of baptism is an outward sign, an act of obedience to the word of God of an inward change. As a child of the Lord God Almighty, the relationship with the Father God is developed as time is spent reading the Old and New Testaments. The Father God has a purpose for man and always will be strongly desirous of having a relationship with all who choose to come to him.

The first thing every good lawyer must do is read the Bible from cover to cover. The Old Testament has so much that it reveals about life and things we all should know and understand about God's plan and purpose and the fulfillment of that purpose. This can be found in the first five books of the Old Testament. The New Testament is the fulfillment of the Old Testament law and fulfilled biblical prophecy.

Just as Jon spent time with his earthly father and was able to know him, he spent time reading the word of God. He learned of the Heavenly Father, the Lord Jesus, and the Holy Ghost. Jon read daily two chapters from the Old Testament, one chapter from the New Testament, one chapter in Psalms, and a chapter in Proverbs to correspond with the day of the month. Jon read through the Old Testament in 9 months. He read through the New Testament in 6 months. Many were the times he read Genesis to Malachi and Matthew through Revelation.

Chapter Six

It was now June 2, and the horse that was to pull the wagon shifted from one foot to another as it was showing an impatient stance. The local neighbor, Mr. Johnson, was going to travel to Kansas City, Missouri, to take a load of corn—his entire crop minus seed corn needed for planting that he had kept from the previous year's harvest. He had taken a gamble hoping for higher prices, and it had paid big dividends.

This wagon with its load of corn would pay him twice the amount per bushel its twin received just 6 months prior. He had even purchased some winter corn from a man in another county who had come pleading to Mr. Johnson that he needed to sell some corn. It was a financial matter of great need.

This man had fallen on some hard times and needed the money to pay his General Store bills and clear some debt on farm implement equipment. The sale of his corn had paid his debts and gave him some money to sustain his family through the winter. The man had kept just enough seed corn to plant in the spring.

The other local farmers were all the Nay Sayers. "You will lose money. You are making the mistake of a life time, a really big, big mistake."

"I prayed," said farmer Johnson. "I have tithed, and I have sown financial seed for this crop. I believe I must do this. My Lord will bless me." He had attended the Assembly of God Church all his life.

Jon had helped load the corn sacks into the wagon and would help unload when they arrived in Kansas City, Missouri, at the mill. The wagon was now completely loaded and ready to leave. His work and assistance were in exchange for a ride to the Kansas City Train Station. Jon's plan was to catch a train from Kansas City, Kansas, west to Colorado.

Excitement was in the air—the anticipation of big profits for farmer Johnson who was more than a happy man. He had kept this last wagonload of corn nicely stored in 100-pound sacks in his barn. In the barn was the seed corn purchased from the man in the adjacent county. Many of the local farmers would need more seed corn to complete their spring planting. Johnson had that product stored safely away in the large red barn for future sales and profit.

The trip from Lamar to Kansas City's large grain mills along the rail road tracks was a slow and hot 120 miles. Both men were thankful when they rolled into the open area across from the long wooden loading dock. Mr. Johnson skillfully backed the wagon up against the loading dock with one of the many large doors close to the end marked "Office." Jon pulled on his leather gloves and was prepared for unloading the large sacks of corn.

A small man with glasses, a vest, and a tie appeared on the dock with a clipboard and asked Jon if he could open one of the sacks and give him some of the corn for testing. Jon quickly did as the man asked, and he was gone as quickly as he had appeared. Jon had just unloaded the large over-sized wagon's cargo on the dock when he was asked to help another hired man to reload the corn sacks into three wagons that were just being backed up to the dock. The drivers helped place the remaining corn sacks in two smaller wagons. With gloved hands, the men made quick work of the loading.

Jon had his work now completed. The wagon was empty except for the personal items of both men. He sat on the wagon seat and waited for Mr. Johnson who finally came out of the office.

After he had climbed up on the wagon's seat, he just sat there smiling. "Jon, you will not believe what just happened. I have to tell someone before I bust and scream my head off in pure out-of-control excitement. It's just 2:30 in the afternoon, and my business is almost completed. Praise the Lord! Thank you, Jesus, for the blessings of God in my life. Hallelujah, Hallelujah! From my mouth to God's ear," he said.

The Johnson family all attended the Assembly of God Church in Lamar, Missouri. The family was well spoken of, and it was said of them to be very religious folk. We Dalton's were Methodists. It has been said "Methodists are a lot like the Baptists, except the Methodists can read." When I hear such talk about

Methodists, I always say, "Well, it's true; I surely must have read that somewhere."

Mr. Johnson continued, "I must tell you what happened. It's almost more than a man could ever hope to experience. I went inside, and I told the clerk at the desk who I was and what I had in my wagon. I was almost immediately approached by a man who was standing to my right. He said, 'Excuse me, sir, may I talk with you before you sell your corn to the mill.' He was a grain and feed buyer for a conglomerate organization that was in need of grain, specifically seed corn. They have contracts with many large grain suppliers and have a high demand for many crops in a five-state area. They were promised a shipment from the mill. Their product was sold to another customer by mistake and was not available for this man's company. I was taken into the office of the president of the Kansas City Grain, Seed and Feed Mill. The man from the Commodity Suppliers of America talked to the president of the mill. I had met the owner last year, and we exchanged pleasantries."

"My corn was checked, and it was some of the best seed they had seen. Almost every sack of my corn was needed to fill this grain salesman's orders for two of his clients. My shipment would be used to fill this man's orders and keep a high dollar contract account that could eventually cause their business to go to another company—not to mention the possibility of breach of contract. My corn and my arrival, exactly at this time and place, saved this man's company thousands of dollars in lost sales, profits, and the possibility of losing a valuable customer."

"In short, I was paid the premium price for my corn. More profit because it tested so high. I was also paid a bonus for future contract business in appreciation for being able to supply product as I did. I signed a contract with the mill for 5 years with assured possibility of contract renewal. I also agreed to sell my future crops and be a confidential supplier for the Commodity Supplier of America exclusively. I have a copy of the contract in the pocket of my coat. I was given a letter of assurance from the company to the bank used by the Kansas City Grain, Seed and Feed. I was paid cash for the delivery of the corn. I have that payment separate in my grip. I also have a draft in my grip that is payment for the bonus—a premium amount paid to me for future grain sales to Commodity Suppliers of America Grain, Seed & Feed Company. The home office is based here in Kansas City. I agreed to be a representative for the mill in southern Missouri and eastern Kansas. I will be trained and introduced to the territory by the company representative who just hired me. I will be called a Dealer Representative to locate wheat, barley, corn, and many crops to meet the demand of this company and their many customers."

"I have a company expense account for reimbursement of expenses in doing business. No, wait, he said, 'in conducting business, you will incur expenses.' He actually used the word 'incur.' I learned a new word today, 'incur.' Let me say this correctly, I will incur expenses in conducting business for the CSofAGS&F Company. That is the Commodity Suppliers of America Grain, Seed & Feed Company." Then Mr. Johnson looked at Jon with a forced humorous expression, and then he could not help but to laugh. Then they both started to laugh.

Mr. Johnson said, "In light of my new employment opportunity, I insist on paying you, Jon, very well for your time. Rather than work in exchange for your ride to Kansas City and a trip to the train depot, which was more than a fair proposition for the work and the time involved, I have decided your pay for assisting me in delivery of product. I am now the Dealer Rep, thanks to my new employer." Mr. Johnson now insisted that Jon accompany him to a local restaurant for a steak. The restaurant was well known in Kansas City as "Bill of Fare," and its specialty was excellent steak prepared to your specific taste. Well, that was the name at the top of the menu posted by the door—"Bill of Fare."

Jon was more than pleased with anticipation of a steak dinner. The restaurant was near the downtown stockyards and was nearly full when the two men arrived. The restaurant was a great experience. The young waiter or food server, as he was called, was very informative. They learned "Bill of Fare" was another name for menu. The term "ala carte" was individual dishes (servings—portions) for specific prices. The strangest term "Prix Fixe" was a fixed meal at a fixed price.

Mr. Johnson inquired of a good hotel in walking distance from the train depot. Upon our arrival at the hotel, he paid for the night's lodging. "I need to make sure you are well cared for. I'll stay with you until you are safe aboard your train. I made a promise to your maw and paw, 'I'll see to it Jon is safely on the train to Colorado.' I am a man of my word."

"I have another very good idea that will pay you future dividends. There was a large bank very close to the hotel and the train depot. Jon, you need to come with me into the bank. I want to do something for you," said Mr. Johnson. The two men stood just inside the large doors of the bank and looked for what must have been a suspicious period of time. A man approached the gawking pair and asked if he could be of assistance.

"We are here to open bank accounts," said Mr. Johnson. "Where do we need to go to have such a service?"

The young man said, "Come this way," and turned and moved in the direction of a large desk. Placing his hands on one of the large stuffed chairs, "Sit here, gentlemen. I'll have someone come and take care your needs."

A tall man with pointed features finally arrived. "Hello, I am Mr. Charles Tremaine Sinclair. Am I right that the two of you want to open checking accounts?"

"That's right, Sir, that is exactly what we intend to do," said Mr. Johnson. "I have a contract with the Commodity Suppliers of America and a letter from the office of the president, a Mr. Elzie D. Montgomery, of the Kansas City Grain, Seed & Feed Company. I have this draft or check, and I would like to open a personal account for myself and also a personal checking account for Mr. Jon Dalton."

"O my, Mr. Dalton, could he possibly be related to the Daltons who are such a menace to so many banks in the southwest?" said the assistant smiling and pointing his finger.

"This Mr. Dalton—no, no, Sir. He is of no relation to anyone remotely connected to those men, I assure you," said Mr. Johnson.

The bank clerk took the contract, the letter, and the draft and read quietly to himself. When he finally looked up, he said, "Well, Mr. Johnson and Mr. Dalton, no relationship to the bank robbers," as he continued to hold the papers and fiddled with them, holding them in his hands nervously tapping the bottom edges of the papers on his desk. "Just how is it I can be of help to you?"

"I would like a personal checking account for myself and Mr. Dalton. I would like to open the accounts from the proceeds from this draft. Mr. Dalton will have an account starting with a $10 deposit." Mr. Johnson smiled and said, "My gift to you, Jon. No thanks necessary."

"The remainder of the funds will be deposited into my account, less some walking around money. Say $40 in gold and silver coins should be enough."

"That should not be a problem. With your contract and the letter of introduction, you are a private contractor of the corporation. This bank is the exclusive bank for the Kansas City Grain, Seed & Feed Company," said the clerk.

"May I suggest the secured savings account for Mr. Dalton that will offer interest paid on the monthly balance in the account? This account also offers the feature of being able to make as many withdrawals as needed in any calendar month without penalty."

"Mr. Johnson, may I suggest a checking and a savings account? If you maintain a savings account balance as we have listed here in this pamphlet, there would be no charge to your account for service. We can offer you a line of credit with the balance to remain over the initial deposit of $200, and you will be able to borrow against your balance and repay within a 30-day period from withdrawal date and pay no interest."

"Mr. Johnson, that's a feature many of our customers enjoy. Just draw out funds whenever you need. However, there might be some penalty and effect on interest for early withdrawal from the secured savings or interest charged if repayment does not fall within the 30-day time limit. The interest is minimal, but the feature we offer is necessary for company representatives who need to purchase product and deliver it to the mill in 30 days or less. It's all right here in this brochure."

It was just under 20 minutes when both Mr. Johnson and Jon were standing on the street again, and this time both men were all smiles.

Chapter Seven

The next morning they walked to the train depot where Jon would soon board the Union Pacific train. Mr. Johnson handed Jon an envelope and said "There's a letter and some money from your folks. They insisted you take it and keep it in a safe place if you need it for your trip west. I am so pleased you are doing what you are doing—going to Colorado following your dreams."

"I would like to pray for you now. We have about 30 minutes before you need to board the train." Mr. Johnson prayed for Jon as they stood in the large train station. When he finally said "Amen," he told Jon that we have not because we ask not. "Do you have a Bible?" asked Mr. Johnson.

"I do have a Bible; it's in my bag. My mother and father gave me this Bible when I graduated from my education. I have a diploma," said Jon. He felt awkward now that he had made reference to the diploma.

Mr. Johnson then said, "I was very impressed to give you this Bible I had at home. It is the King James Version of the Bible, and I feel I must give it to you. I went through and transcribed many of the notes and the information I have in my personal Bible. I have made notes on top, down the sides, and along the bottom of some of the pages. I have been so very blessed, and I know the Lord God Almighty wants to bless you as well."

"In the front pages that were blank, I have listed verses concerning salvation, water baptism, infilling with the Spirit called filling of the Holy Spirit with the evidence of praying in tongues. I have used the specific words used in God's Word. I have also covered the laying on of hands with expectation of total healing and deliverance."

"I have a hand-written copy of the words from a message I preached about this teaching. I had my wife make the copy. She has far better handwriting than I do. I asked her if she would make another copy when I realized you and I would be traveling together to Kansas City." Mr. Johnson was now reading aloud what his wife had so clearly and patiently handwritten on the pages he was holding.

Jesus taught the disciples about the Holy Ghost or Holy Spirit, the Comforter. The Lord Jesus tells us of the promise of the Holy Spirit, the Comforter. Read John 14:16-17: "I will pray the Father, and he shall give you another comforter, that he may abide with you forever; even the Spirit of truth; whom the world cannot receive, because it seeth him not, neither knoweth him; but ye know him; for he dwelleth with you, and shall be in you." At the time of your salvation when you were born again, the Holy Spirit came to live inside of you. Your spiritual growth started and does not stop. The Holy Spirit of God works in you to be a mature child of God, to know the deep things of God. Read for yourself I Corinthians 2:1-16, revealing wisdom, the spiritual man to conform to the image of Jesus Christ. Romans 8:29: "For whom he did foreknow, he also did predestinate to be conformed to the image of his son, that he might be the first born among many brethren." Romans 12:1-2: "Present your bodies a living sacrifice, Holy, acceptable unto God, which is your reasonable service."

On the day of Pentecost, Acts 2:1-4, these Jewish believers were filled with the Holy Spirit and definitely spoke in tongues for it was heard in many known languages. This is the first of the signs foretold in Mark 16:15-20; read verses 17-18, "In my name they shall cast out devils; they shall speak with new tongues . . . they shall lay hands on the sick and they shall recover. In Acts 1:3, Jesus showed himself alive. Acts 1:4, Jesus' instruction "being assembled together, commanded them that they should not depart Jerusalem but wait for the promise of the Father." Acts 1:5: "For John truly baptized with water; but you shall be baptized with the Holy Ghost not many days hence." In Acts 1:13-14, "Among those present the eleven apostles, these all continued with one accord in prayer and supplication, with the women, and Mary the mother of Jesus, and with his brethren." (The number of names together were about an hundred and twenty.) This was the start, the beginning, of the New Testament church age.

Peter and John were sent out to Samaria in Acts 8:14-17. Verse 14: "Now when the apostles who were in Jerusalem heard that Samaria had received the word of God, they sent unto them Peter and John. Who, when they came down, prayed for them, that they might receive the Holy Ghost." (For as yet he was fallen upon none of them, only they were baptized in the name of Jesus.) Verse 17: "Then laid they their hands on them, and they received the Holy Ghost." Some argue it is not mentioned here that they did speak in tongues. I have laid hands on many people. I prayed, and they prayed to be filled with the Holy Ghost and most spoke instantly in tongues. Some do not speak instantly, but later in time they receive a prayer language. Some do not. I believe all are filled as they pray. I also believe those who do not have a prayer language have other gifts manifest in their lives.

Simon the Sorcerer, Acts 8:18-19. Start by reading verse 18: "And when Simon (the sorcerer, see verse 9) saw that through laying on of the apostles' hands the Holy Ghost was given, he offered them money." Verse 19: "Saying, give me also this power, that whomsoever I lay hands, he may receive the Holy Ghost." When Simon saw? The Word says you can't see the Holy Ghost. He is a Spirit and cannot be seen with the physical eye. There had to be some physical sign. Otherwise how could Simon know they had received the Holy Ghost? Something obvious that would be apparent to Simon to desire this gift so as to attempt to buy it. All evidence indicated the sign manifested was speaking in tongues. Peter then rebuked him and said Simon was in the Gall of Bitterness and in the bond of iniquity. Simon seemed to not be a child of God. He was fearful and asked Peter to pray for him that none of these things come upon him. I want to believe Peter or another believer did pray for Simon and he became a child of God.

Paul's infilling with the Holy Spirit, Acts 9:10-12, 17. Start with verse 17: "And Ananias went his way, and entered into the house; and putting his hands on him said, Brother Saul, the Lord, even Jesus, that appeared unto thee in the way as thou camest, hath sent me, that thou mightest receive thy sight, and be filled with the Holy Ghost." Paul did receive his sight forthwith and arose and was baptized. Paul didn't speak with tongues at this time, but scripture records Paul did speak in tongues and gave specific instruction at a later time.

Cornelius, a Greek gentile filled with the Holy Ghost, Acts 10:1-48. Cornelius was one of many gentiles, a Greek Jewish proselyte who lived in Caesarea. The word reveals to us that prior to this time the believers in this New Testament church were made up of Jewish converts to a belief in Jesus Christ. Reading Acts 10:1-8, Cornelius had a visitation from an angel with special instructions. He sent three men to Joppa, to call for Simon surnamed Peter, lodging with Simon the Tanner by the seaside. Peter had a vision about what is clean and unclean—a specific instruction from God. While Peter thought on the meaning of the vision, the Spirit said unto him, "Behold three men seek thee. Arise therefore, and get thee down, and go with them, doubting nothing; for I have sent them."

Peter is met by the three men, and on the morrow they are going to the household of Cornelius. Peter, two servants, a soldier, and men from Joppa also accompanied them.

Cornelius had called together his kinsmen and near friends. Cornelius tells Peter of his encounter and instruction by the angel. Peter preached the gospel of Christ to these gentiles for they had need of salvation. Acts 10:44-46: "While Peter yet spake these words, the Holy Ghost fell on all of them which heard the word. And they of the circumcision, which believed, were astonished, as many as came with Peter, because that on the gentiles also was poured out the gift of the Holy Ghost. For they heard them speak with tongues, and magnify God." Lastly verse 47: "Can any man forbid water, that these should not be baptized, which have received the Holy Ghost as well as we?"

Believers are filled with the Spirit in Ephesus. Paul had a mission trip to Ephesus and met believers and introduced them to the Holy Ghost. Acts 19:1-3 and 6-7: "And it came to pass, that, while Apollos was at Corinth, Paul having passed through the upper coasts came to Ephesus and finding certain disciples, he said unto them, have you received the Holy Ghost since you have believed? And they said unto him, we have not so much as heard whether there be any Holy Ghost. And he said unto them, Unto what were you baptized? And they said, Unto John's Baptism." Lastly read verses 6 and 7: "And when Paul had laid his hands upon them, the Holy Ghost came upon them; they spake with tongues and prophesied. And all the men were about twelve."

These believers had never heard of the Holy Ghost. When Paul laid hands on them, the Holy Ghost came upon them, and they spoke with tongues. Each of them prayed in tongues without any waiting. All were filled with the Holy Ghost and spoke with other tongues as the Holy Ghost gave them utterance.

Mr. Johnson asked Jon about his belief in the death, burial, and the resurrection of the Lord Jesus Christ. "You have prayed a prayer for salvation, have you not?" said Mr. Johnson.

"Yes I have," said Jon.

"Would you indulge me and pray again with me aloud?"

"Yes, I was led in a prayer of salvation. I prayed aloud. I understood how I was in need of being Spirit filled with the evidence of praying in tongues."

Mr. Johnson said, "Jon, would you allow me to lead you in an additional prayer to be filled with the Holy Ghost with evidence of a prayer language called tongues. Would you choose as an act of your will, do you desire to be Spirit filled and pray in tongues?"

Jon said, "Yes."

Mr. Johnson then said, "Repeat after me, Father God in Jesus name, fill me with the Holy Spirit of God with evidence of speaking in tongues, that I will have a prayer language. Amen."

Mr. Johnson then said, "Listen to me as I pray in tongues in my prayer language." He then placed his right hand on Jon's stomach and his left hand on Jon's back. He started to pray and release what he said was an anointing to pray in the Spirit and an anointing of empowerment."

Jon felt something really change in him as he prayed. He raised his hands right in the train station and started to pray in a different language. He prayed and laughed and felt so full of joy.

"Well, my boy, you got all I have for you today. Certainly not all of what God has for you in your full life to come. Be open and willing; you are well on the way to receive more than you can think or imagine," said Mr. Johnson.

Jon heard a man with a loud voice yelling, "Last call for trains to all points west—Leavenworth, Salina, Abilene, Fort Hays, all points west to Denver, Colorado, Den-ver, Co-lo-rad-doe—last call. All aboard, all aboard, now leaving through Gate C. ALL ABOARD! LAST CALL!"

"That call is for you, my boy, go now. Your adventure awaits. You are starting the first day of the rest of your life," said Mr. Johnson smiling. They both walked quickly toward the train. Jon took the last two strides up the wooden steps of the train. The train conductor quickly removed the stairs. He walked on into the train car, and looking out of a window, he waved to his friend who now meant far more to him than just Farmer Johnson who gave him a ride to Kansas City.

Jon used the universal sign language for the deaf, and slowly signed: "I love you and I am praying for you; please pray for me."

Mr. Johnson nodded and gave him the thumbs up sign and said "Amen, brother!" loud enough for Jon to hear through the closed train window.

The train lurched, and he made his way to his seat after first stowing his bag in the overhead compartment. The train lurched forward again. After almost losing his balance, he sat slowly down in his seat. He looked around to see if anyone had seen his awkward display, but no one seemed to even be aware he was there. Jon was facing east toward Kansas City as the train was now slowly moving west.

The train increased and gained speed; and in short order, Jon was moving faster than he had ever moved over God's green earth. This was faster and so much more comfortable than the seat on Mr. Johnson's wagon. The large folded quilt placed on the wagon seat made it a tolerable, not an enjoyable ride. The train seat was quite nice, and it made sitting for a long period of time comfortable.

The train it was like being in a machine that was moving from the past into the uncertain and unknown future and in many ways that was exactly what was happening. Inside the train you could sit, read, walk around, and eat—and if needed, you could use the facilities. Jon Dalton was moving from his life in the State of Missouri to a life he had only dreamed of and visualized in his mind. On a trip, Jon would always visualize what the house of the relative would look like when he would eventually arrive. Every time when he arrived, it looked far different than what he had visualized in his mind.

After an hour or so of looking out the windows of the train as the view of the countryside slowly slipped from the present into the past as everything seemed to move past the windows and mystically disappear from his vision, Jon decided to again read the letter from his cousin Frank that gave some arrival instructions when he arrived in the Rocky Mountain town of Central City, Colorado.

You need to mail a letter from the post office in Lamar, Missouri, about a month before you intend to leave from Kansas City on the Union Pacific train. It is hard to determine how long the mail service will take.

When you arrive in Denver, you will need to get a ride to the canyon entrance. You will see to the west two large mesas; stay to the south of both, and follow a well-traveled two-lane rut road or path.

Make sure you can make the date as close to the date in the letter as possible. Upon his arrival in Central City, Colorado, Jon was instructed to go to the Post Office and ask for the Post Master, a Mr. H. J. Sears. He would know when Frank Dalton last checked in for his mail. He usually checked in every Monday, but if Jon was close to the arrival date, Frank would check every Friday as well.

Frank had told Jon that he had been sharing a cabin with three other men. He usually just slept there. It's near Central City, but it might be a little hard to find for someone who is new to the area.

Jon was told the Teller House was easy to find. It's a four-story brick building where he could get a room. The Cyclops Assay Office is just next door to the Teller House. Frank personally knew the owner and told him Jon might come asking for him. Frank told Jon of some cafés and places where he could eat. The restaurant in the Teller House has excellent food, but you will pay more than you would in most of the other places you can buy a meal. Frank suggested a good meal could be had at Dostal Alley and some of the other saloons. The Glory Hole was one of his favorites. The Saint James Episcopal Church was a nice stone building across the street from the Teller House. The pastor was a good man, and he also was acquainted with Frank Dalton.

Chapter Eight

It was the early spring of 1884. Jon was traveling to join his favorite cousin, Mr. Frank Randall Dalton. Every one called him Frank, but some close relatives called him Randy because he preferred the sound and the informal aspect of the name. Jon was on the Union Pacific train to Denver, Colorado. The rail road had provided continuous service since June 24, 1870, 15 years prior to Jon's journey.

A St. Louis city girl on the train was not traveling alone, but with her aunt and uncle who were never seen but apparently in another car. The afternoon into the evening was filled with her talking—what had become a one-person conversation by way of her deductive thinking as she called it. Jon was listening to every word with a natural curiosity having never heard or considered any of what she was saying. After being told of Jon's final destination, she offered to be a pen pal. She said she would write him at General Delivery, Central City, Colorado.

Late in the evening, the girl asked Jon if he would mind if she stayed a little while longer. Instantly after his affirmative answer, she took Jon's hand and pressed it to her cheek then kissed the back of his hand. Turning in her seat toward him, even in the dark Jon could feel her looking directly at him. She moved closer until she kissed Jon on the mouth, slowly gently pressed her mouth to his. This was the first time Jon had been kissed by a woman. Still holding his hand, she turned and placed her head on his shoulder and fell asleep.

The departure of the girl brought Jon a sweet solitude again. For Jon the trip took on a mood of just some time to himself to again enjoy the scenery that was forever passing just outside the train windows—when it was light enough to see it.

The restaurant car was Jon's favorite. The food was a variety of things to try and eat that he had literally never seen nor tasted before, a real delight and food experience. Jon made notes of names and some recipes of what he had eaten and the specific names of some items and how they were spelled, so as to be able to order properly in future restaurants and cafés. Jon truly anticipated every dining experience. It was considered for the most part to be the beginning of a life-long education. Jon was experiencing a part of life in these United States he had never seen before. He was seeing himself in his mind's eye to be or who he thought at the time just who and where he wanted to be.

Chapter Nine

L ike all good things we first experience, the trip to Denver finally came to an end. Jon walked from the train station and up the 16th street of Denver. He stopped and inquired how he would make his way to the fair town of Golden and up the canyon to Central City. The trip from downtown Denver would be on a stagecoach west out to Golden. The Loop—a central location in downtown Denver—then out to Golden. Straight west toward the mountains, Jon rode up on the top seat of the coach where he sat and talked with the driver.

The stagecoach moved along stirring up the fine dust of the two-rut road bed. Jon arrived in the small town of Golden where he had lunch in the Mercantile Restaurant on the main street. The town was literally at the foot of the Rockies. That night he would spend in a boarding house—a suggestion from the stagecoach driver who stayed there himself in the past. The wagon ride or the modified stagecoach ride up the canyon to Black Hawk and on to the final destination of Central City was a long grueling experience that many a traveler was glad to see completed.

A traveler could also catch a ride on one of the many ore wagons making its way up the canyon. It was a full day of travel up the canyon with many bridges to cross. The trip was slow and very uncomfortable as the road made its winding way up the canyon. The bridges of the many river crossings were crossed with the payment of a toll fee—a cost of 2 to 5 pennies or more for each passenger in the stagecoach or the large ore wagon. In the 1880's, the time needed to travel the 17 miles from Central City to Golden, Colorado, was a full day.

A rail road was eventually the length of the entire canyon to move the gold and silver ore down the canyon. This passenger and ore train was used until it was decided by the State of Colorado that it needed to be replaced.

The rail road tracks were removed and the rail road bed became the route for the present day Highway 6 up the canyon to Black Hawk and Central City. The old train roadbed can still be seen in just a very few locations in the canyon. The remarkable stonework can still be seen from a few key locations in the once famous canyon. This project was completed in the year 1952. Three tunnels were dug, and Highway 6 moves thousands of cars daily up and down this canyon.

The Gilpin Hotel was built in 1869. The address is 111 Main Street, Black Hawk, Colorado. The bronze plaque mounted by the hotel entrance will verify "Built in 1869."

This is now the year 1884. Jon witnessed a man standing on Main Street drunk and shooting at the buildings until his last shot was fired, and he walked slowly down Main Street.

The Bull Durham building in Black Hawk still stands on the corner of Gregory and Main Street. The building's physical address is 100 Main Street. This historical location would be sporting the same name and address for the next hundred and twenty plus years. Directly across the street from the Bull Durham, you will see 101 Main Street. This address is currently the location of the Fitzgerald's Casino, Black Hawk, Colorado, established in the year 2000.

Chapter Ten

Jon and Frank would share living accommodations with other miners; and when traveling, they would use a tent for the summer. Basic equipment included a pan for gold and pots for cooking.

Frank had ventured down the creek from Black Hawk believing the heavier gold dust would have moved downstream for centuries, and this was where he originally found his first real success. The physical demands were many for the hours needed to produce a substantial amount of gold dust—a sore back, aching knees, and hands that become numb and stiff from the cold water were only some of the demanding payment gold took for its extraction from the stream. That's when Frank built and used a water-driven sluice box. This increased the gold production and was operated in an upright standing position. What a relief for the back and knees.

There was the traditional fall trip to Denver. The high country was not the place to live during the fierce winter snows of the Colorado mountains. The boarding house where they both decided to live was comfortable and demanded payment every month usually from October or November through March or April depending on when the snow would start to melt. The spring runoff made the river in the canyon almost impassable.

Frank said, "We will both need to find a job to pay the bills. We will not tap the money from the gold dust we worked so hard to pan from the cold mountain streams." The jobs they took more than paid the winter bills with usually enough to make a good grub stake for the spring return to the hills, "to them thar gold fields."

The winter job came easy for Jon, the aggressive salesman. Jon heard of the job and the opportunity in Louisville, Colorado, to work in the coal mine. The job was actually wagon delivery of the "black gold." These coal mines were only mined part of the year, starting in the early fall, through the early spring to provide for the demand of the precious coal. The original Welsh Coal Mine was started with heavy mining in 1877. It was called the Northern Coal Foundation. The town of Louisville was named by many of the early residents, such as the family or specifically by a man named Louis Navatny, said to be the founder of the town. It was incorporated in 1882. There were people living in the area when it was an unincorporated area and the town was yet to be organized with a town charter and legally placed on an official ballot and voted to be a town. Louisville would have been a company town if other mines were not discovered and mined in the general area.

The coal mined and delivered all across the Front Range placed a need for drivers and hailers to deliver the black gold into Denver and the surrounding towns. The Arapahoe County town of Littleton was increasing in population and was the largest town in the county. Another town literally at the foot of the Rockies was Boulder, founded in 1860 and incorporated in 1873.

The winters in Denver were cold, and snow coming fast and furious was a part of the Colorado winter. The winter in the high mountains with the deep snow made travel virtually impossible for the coldest months of the year. The inability to mine or pan for gold due to the frozen ground and the ice-covered creek made enterprising men look to the Front Range or down below as it was called for employment and housing in the freezing cold winter months. Black Hawk and Central City were literally snowed in and travel was cut off. The frozen ground stopped far more than just the mining.

The coal mine in Louisville would offer work during the winter months. A delivery schedule for a one-man coal wagon was good money. It was cold, hard, and dirty work. Monday through Saturday arrive at work at 4 a.m., hitch up the horses to the wagons, and start moving as soon as possible. The coal yard was empty by 5 a.m. Wagons moved out to every area of the front range delivering to the towns. The graveyard shift had filled all the wagons, checked out, and were somewhere sleeping until the next night when their work would start all over again.

Deliver as many loads as possible to local customers. The coal was usually stored in the basement coal bin or in a shed near the house. All the towns of any size had a local warehouse where the coal was stored until it could be delivered to the homes of the customers. Jon, working with the management, told the company president that a small partial load with free delivery should be offered to new residents with anticipation they surely would desire a larger monthly delivery throughout the winter. Jon told the management that they needed a wagon ready to deliver emergency loads if a customer needed more coal product for whatever reason—if the weather was extremely cold or their supply was running low. The emergency delivery price was a little higher per ton, with complimentary no delivery fee. However, the higher price would also cover any delivery fee.

Jon was in charge of the Emergency and New Resident complementary accounts. He would schedule deliveries for the front range with his hand-picked men for the special account teams. His company was the only coal supplier, but they needed to appear to offer customer service. Jon's drivers would offer to deliver a final partial load in the late spring for the fall, but this rarely happened.

There was a need to have coal in the basement of every home from the most meager to the more prosperous residents and finer homes in the area. Many stoves in the kitchens used coal, so fewer men were needed for summer and early autumn. The company was always looking for drivers and wagons in the late summer and early fall for the stocking of the warehouses. Jon was always available and was depended on by the company for his good business and organization skills.

There were stories told in the later years during prohibition when liquor was forbidden about the many caves and tunnels that were eventually dug by the Louisville coal miners from homes nearby to the basements of some of the previous taverns and saloons. The windows of the saloons were boarded up, so if someone were in these buildings late at night drinking and playing poker, no one would be the wiser.

The Blue Parrot was a restaurant in Louisville started in the early 1900's, the exact date was most likely in the year 1908 or 1909. Prior to this most notable Blue Parrot, there were other cafés that would offer lunches and dinners to go. Jon would load up with coal, head out on the delivery, and stop by the No Name Café—another café with lunches and dinners to go. They would buy lunches and dinners to go to eat on the road. The food was excellent and at an increased cost with some profit for the restaurant.

Many valuable contacts were made and listed as they collected information for our young entrepreneurs. A list was made of the most successful and influential business people who might respond to a contact and a time of questioning. We made our list of bankers and successful men and women educated from colleges and schools. We were on a search for ideas, careers, and possible investments from whatever varied place it might come. Jon and Frank would ask those on their list if they might buy a lunch or a dinner meal for them in exchange for business and career information, questions, and answers. This gave both men many and varied insights into many areas of future endeavor for the possible financial betterment of both men. Gold had been a dream—now from years of panning, a reality. Jon and Frank decided make a living with what they could do best.

The master plan was decided by both men and would most assuredly become a reality. They planned to save enough money (their banker called investment capital) to buy a boarding house in Denver. The secondary or follow-up plan was to eventually buy a second and a third house with room and board accommodations. The kitchen would be worked with a live-in cook/assistant manager. They already had a mental list of women who wanted to do the work. The cook would provide a dual role as assistant boarding house manager. She and her family would have free room and board and receive a salary for her services.

The size of the houses needed to be large enough to accommodate as many boarders as possible, two stories with main floor and upstairs rooms. The basement would need a boiler for heating, with additional space for storage. A café could be operated out of the kitchen, and the living room could double as a large dining room for additional customers. The parlor could be a meeting room for guests. The front door could have a built-in counter in the entryway to check guests who pay in advance to stay in the boarding house. The counter and entryway with chairs was a place to ask customers to wait before they are seated in the café dining room. The counter would serve as a place to rent a room, pay for lodging, pay the bill for a meal, and leave messages for guests who were out. "How does that read?" said Jon to Frank.

Chapter Eleven

A plan was written out and set in motion for the future. They would both work this winter for the coal mine. All money not needed for expenses was to be saved for a house to purchase and convert into a boarding house. Eventually a much larger building would be purchased—a hotel with as many rooms that could be constructed or added. With the constant influx of people into Denver, many were looking for a temporary place to live.

A tailor shop could be operated from one of the houses with a crew of seamstresses to make clothes, shirts, pants, and dresses. With the proper contacts, a tailor could make and produce suits for business and professional men. There will always be a demand for work clothes and every day clothes. These seamstresses can be found and hired to make everyday work clothes.

The boarding house would offer clean, comfortable rooms with bath accommodations, a nice café, and eventually a restaurant in the same building.

Buy a home and convert it into a boarding house. The profits from jobs and the money from the mining efforts would be a down payment. The year 1885 was the year Frank and Jon became home owners or property owners. The plan was to buy it in the late summer, change any needed construction of the house, and rent out the extra rooms to men who had worked with them up in the mines who would need a place to stay in Denver during the cold winter months.

They would hire a cook and a washerwoman who would provide laundry services. This was a room and board opportunity with as many rooms as they were able to purchase outright. It was considered, however, not as profitable to find a homeowner who wanted to convert their home into a boarding house or rent out one or two rooms. The men would offer management and advertise to fill the always-available rooms.

The second year 1886, the plan was again to buy real estate. The First Bank of Denver was the mortgage holder for Jon and Frank's room and board establishment. The conversion of property into a boarding house was a profitable business, showing a monthly profit; and a track record was established with the bank. This would be important for purchasing the second larger property. The bank had their proven financial track record and would be more open to loan money to purchase property with the same anticipation. The profits from the renters paid the house mortgage payments and a good living with profits for more local investments.

Always have available as many rooms to rent as possible. If all rooms are full, find a place for a guest to stay even in the home of local residents who had decided to rent a spare room. If all else fails, check with other boarding houses in the area and recommend them. Keep up a favorable relationship with businesses that can and will trade services. Present two complimentary free food coupons and vouchers for future times for a meal and surely spend a night or longer at the Dalton's Boarding House. Jon was always thinking about how to do things better and more efficiently. Business was very good for the Dalton boys as the seemingly never ending stream of people from the east came west to find their fortune.

The third year 1887, another property was purchased. The fourth year 1888, four more boarding houses were added to their real estate collection.

Someone was always looking for a room—demand was high. One family would squeeze into a single room; and two or three men in a room was not uncommon. All were glad to have a place to stay. Most were happy just to have a room and not be out in the street or under a bridge as it were, although few were ever denied if they had the money to pay. Dalton's Boarding House, "A clean room and good food—all for affordable prices."

The cook would pack a lunch for each guest who requested one for a small charge. The Daltons decided to hire an entire family to operate and manage one of the boarding houses. The husband was in charge of general maintenance of the property, fixing and repairing whatever was needed. The overall operation was usually done by the wife who would rent the rooms, collect the money, cook and manage the kitchen and the laundry. The parents paid their children for any work they provided. The children were sometimes limited in their availability to work, usually after school and on the weekends.

They would offer washing and ironing of clothes for a fee, if requested by a guest. The sheets were changed every day for guests who stayed only one night. Bedding was changed weekly for the guest who stayed for a month or longer. Some were considered permanent residents. Although no formal contract was ever signed, everyone rented week to week or just for one night or more. The clothes laundry for the guests was a service that saw marginal profits, but it all added up and that made its way to the bottom line. The exchange for the work of the live-in managers was free rent and a small salary paid monthly. The husband usually had a job, and the wife and the daughters were mostly employed at the boarding house. Usually only the evening meals were included with the price of the room or sold separately at a fair price. The wives and daughters were usually hired as waitresses, kitchen help, and housemaids.

Chapter Twelve

Chen and Frank met in Central City. Frank had convinced Chen to go to Denver and relocate his laundry business. The greater potential for a large volume of business could grow with the needs of Denver residents and would give many years of increased profit for Chen's family business. The gold town of Central City was up in the mountains and with some initial success, it was apparent this business could vanish with the possibility of the gold rush ending.

This prairie town was originally called Auraria. Later renamed Denver City, it was the second choice for the state capitol. Central City and Leadville were also being considered to be the capitol of Colorado. The original county seat was first located in Golden, Colorado, but later moved to Denver. The city of Denver was named after the Kansas Territorial Governor.

This growing city on the Platte River would be a far greater opportunity for steady growth. Chen could bring his family to Denver and increase the family-owned business. The Central City winters diminished his work due to the town being snowed in for months. His wife and children could help in the business far sooner without the interference of the harsh winters. The possibility of opening a second location that his children could operate independent from the original location was a great idea, but that was not a possibility in Central City.

The plan was finally decided during the first winter. Chen decided to take Frank's advice. The plan was to work the spring and the summer and set aside as much profit as possible to assist with the cost of relocation. Finally a day in late July was selected, long before the fall snows would arrive and while the canyon was open for travel. Frank had found two men with a wagon who were willing, for the right price, to take Chen, his family, and all his equipment down the canyon to the banks of the Platte River.

A large tent was erected for the start of his soon to be thriving laundry business. Chen wanted to operate the best laundry in the Market, Lawrence, Larimer, and Wazee Streets area. Frank kept a lookout for a building to become available. Then Frank and Chen made an offer on the building for the laundry business. This happened by mid October, just 4 months after the first day the tent was erected along the bank of the South Platte River. The building would get Chen's family and the laundry inside for the winter and allow the business to operate every day of the year come rain, snow, or sunshine.

Chen called his laundry the Dalton Laundry and told everyone he was the manager. Mr. Dalton, he boss—he owner. Chen operating manager. Smiling and bowing he would say, "Thank you for your business. Mister Dalton thanks you." This was not true. Frank had no financial involvement, but the secret was never revealed to anyone, not even the wife and children of Chen. The days when racial persecution came upon many oriental businesses, Chen was never mistreated in any way. Unfortunately, this was not true of many other oriental business owners. The Celestials, Orientals, and Devil Foreigners faced some severe persecution.

Many of the ladies who lived in the boarding houses were single women or wives of the men who were friends of Frank or Jon, and they found work with Chen. Chen asked Frank if he could put up signs in the boarding houses—"Seamstress needed for mending and dress manufacturing." With patterns, many dresses were completed and sold from the displays in the windows of the Dalton Laundry. With more patterns ordered from Chicago, men's suits were made and placed on display for sale.

The laundry service was included and provided by Chen for anyone in the boarding houses of Frank and Jon Dalton. This was a valued feature for all the guests. Chen charged his regular laundry fee, and he offered a no-charge pickup and delivery service for the guests of the boarding houses due to his respect and appreciation for Frank. This special service caught on, and Chen picked up other customers just for the free pickup and delivery. He said his employees deserved free laundry service, so he offered it as a bonus for work provided. Chen was a smart enterprising businessman with an eye for innovation and originality.

The female seamstresses contributed a significant influence on Chen's business. Frank never told anyone he was not the owner or a part owner of Chen's businesses. Frank would say "What we have here is an American tradition of good hard work and customer service." The reason behind the friendship was never revealed. It was the secret of secrets between two friends. Chen would many times bow and back away from Frank and say, "Yes, Boss, I will see to it. Anything you say, Boss, Mr. Frank Dalton."

Chen opened a tailor shop called "Dalton—Men's Clothier and Tailor Services." He used the seamstresses to operate the store and communicate with the customers. The ladies were a great success and would take the measurements of the customers. The large selection of bolt material available could be selected from the swatches on display for the manufacturing of suits, shirts, and pants completed and ready for pick up by the customer between 4 and 6 p.m. the third day after measurement. Standard sizes were also available from inventory hanging on racks for instant purchase. The demand was all but never ending as the clothes were sold and the racks were replenished and waiting for the next customers. Chen would say, "Happy to see good sales. Boss be happy. Mr. Frank Dalton, good boss."

Chen had designed a full service tailor shop, with rooms to manufacture the suits for the men and dresses for the ladies. Eventually a second line of manufactured clothes were ordered and shipped in from Chicago. The shirts, pants, dresses, underwear, and accessories were ordered from the best stores in Chicago, St. Louis, and Kansas City. The brand names were complete with labels "Men's Wear" and "Work Clothes" for the business casual and mining workforce. There were special double-lined pants with reinforced knees and shirts with a gabardine lining like a coat with reinforced elbows. Chen also ordered cloth from the orient and made the most magnificent dresses and suits for Denver City's elite.

Street front homes were purchased and converted by the Daltons. Some were rented out to businesses that would operate a bakery, barber shop, butcher shop, or general store in the building. The monthly rent more than paid the mortgage payment for the investment property. They built specially designed storage rooms deep in the lower rooms of the basement for storing ice. They had first boiled water and then had frozen it during the long cold Colorado winters. The ice was sold in the spring and early summer to restaurants and saloons.

Some of the local businesses were renting only the main floor of the street front buildings. The upstairs rooms were converted into rental space for employees or anyone who needed a room. The back-door entrance and access seemed to have little or no effect in keeping the rooms rented.

Frank and Chen discussed a boarding house which would be purchased by Chen, and the rooms would be available for the Celestials (Chinese emigrants) who were new arrivals to the Denver area. Chen and his family would virtually live for free and his tailor business could be separately located in one or more of the rooms. A main street or business front location for the property would not be necessary. A cook and manager who spoke the language of some of the new arrivals could manage the house and live rent-free in exchange for the services of collecting rent, renting rooms, and cooking foods more palatable to the Celestials' tastes and expectations.

Chen and Frank were both aware of the specific foods some of the Celestials ate and enjoyed. These foods were prepared in the kitchen in this separate boarding house. Then the oriental café idea came up, and the parlor dining area was used as seating. The large wrap-around porch on the Chen Boarding House was screened in; and breakfast, lunch, and dinner were served on the porch also, weather permitting.

Eventually large windows were special ordered and placed all around and the complete structure was available for year round elegant Chinese dinning. The interior was converted to Chinese decor, and it became one of the best oriental restaurants in the Denver area. Many individuals who owned restaurants in Chicago and Kansas City came and marveled at the design, elegance, and atmosphere displayed in the restaurant. The food was a varied montage of entries served and always available. Chefs from all parts of the world who came were impressed with this elegant Chinese restaurant. Chen insisted on the name: **THE IMPERIAL PALACE—A fine Chinese restaurant.**

The menus were printed with a color and design that were a work of art. One evening a man came and visited the restaurant. It was later determined he was a very wealthy restaurant owner from South America. He was looking for an idea or theme he could recreate in his country. Chen's restaurant was unlike anything he had seen. His desire was to have an identical menu or Bill of Fare as Chen had.

This man asked his waiter if he could take the menu when they left the restaurant and look over the array of selections, divine descriptions, and remarkable drawings of the exact placement for featured items. The waiter approached Chen and asked if the menu could be taken. Chen approached the table and introduced himself. The man requesting a menu introduced himself using his full given name and commented upon the excellent design of the restaurant menu. Chen asked the man what country he was from. A short conversation between the two men was exchanged about the man's interest in Chen's restaurant and Mr. Esmaralda's restaurants in Brazil.

Chen asked his older daughter who could read and write English to come to the table. Chen took a menu and asked his daughter to write a statement inside the first page of the menu, *This menu can be copied, duplicated, and used to any extent Mr. Carlos Bosco Esmaralda desires for his private, personal, or professional use.* Then Chen signed his name and Frank Dalton's name. Then Chen asked his daughter to sign her name; after her name, she wrote Restaurant Manager.

Chen told the man from Brazil that he and his party would dine as his personal guests. He would ask when the duplicate of the menu was printed in Portuguese if Mr. Esmaralda would be so kind as to send one menu for Chen's approval. Chen handed his card with the restaurant address printed on to Mr. Esmaralda. With this final comment, Chen excused himself and walked to the guest seating station and spoke with the headwaiter, and signed the ticket for the party from Brazil. Chen then walked back to the table, placed his hands together and nodded to the table, said "Your party enjoy everything compliments of house. May I select bottle of best wine for you to enjoy, yes, yes? Mr. Carlos Bosco Esmaralda, you honor me, flatter me, with your request to include menu in your restaurant. Please come tomorrow at 10 a.m. to talk with chef and exchange recipes, yes? Good time is 10 a.m.—fine time for you?" Carlos stood and took Chen's hands in both of his and spoke in low tones. Chen was smiling and nodding his head until Carlos released his hands and slowly moved back to his chair. Chen nodded again, then slowly turned and disappeared into the kitchen.

The Celestials came from all parts of the orient, and word spread of Chen's boarding house. It was not long until some of the Celestials were asking for Chen and Frank to open another restaurant. A third larger building was found, and this structure showcased the beauty and interior design for oriental cuisine and dining. It was an innovation before its time in the young city of Denver, Colorado. However, soon after its grand opening, a company from back east made a financial offer Chen and Frank were not able to refuse.

When Frank and Jon decided to leave Colorado and return home to Lamar, Missouri, they signed the largest and most well built boarding house over to Chen. The bank placed the mortgage in his name, and Chen and his family lived in the building until his children were married and gone. He eventually sold all his business interests, returned to his homeland, and lived out his senior years there with his wife. Chen's children and family all attended the 50-year wedding anniversary of Chen and his wife in their homeland. Chen and his family were from one of the poorest provinces in China.

All of the Chen children were educated in the U.S. and spoke English and their native language fluently. All of the children finished high school, and all but one attended college, graduated, and were degreed professionals. Their grade point average was usually all "A's." The ability to strive for excellence and perfection was inherent in all of the Chen children.

Chen had a picture taken of Frank Dalton, and he kept it on the wall behind the cash register and referred to the owner and proprietor "Mr. Frank Dalton, my Boss, he appreciate your business. You come again, please." Chen, his business, and his family were never shown any discourtesy; and no persecution ever came to their family during the time from the moving of the business from Black Hawk to Denver and through the years until Chen left with his wife and returned home to China.

The total amount of monies sent home to family and relatives and the money Chen amassed was never revealed. This frugal man lived out his final days in one of the nicest homes built in the province where Chen was born in China. He was always very frugal, but he still gave much to many during his final years. A large inheritance even in today's standards was left to each of his children and his grandchildren.

When we consider the economic conditions of the country in the time in which Chen lived and the total amount of money he made, it will probably never be completely determined. Chen never divulged any amount of the totals he made from the many enterprises he created and developed for Mr. Boss Frank Dalton. Well, maybe except to Frank, and Frank was always a tightlipped man when he wanted to be. The bank had records, but they were never divulged to anyone. In reality, Frank never received a penny from Chen from the profits of his many businesses. Frank's name was used only to protect Chen from the persecution that some of the Celestials experienced.

Chen sent letters to Frank up to and after he and his wife returned to China.

Chen asked Frank many times in his letters to visit China. Frank always wanted to, but he never did. Chen sent pictures to Frank of his homes in the town and the province where he lived.

"I have a problem pronouncing the words and the names written on the pictures, but the beauty of China cannot be compared to anyplace I have ever seen," said Frank to Jon as they looked at the many pictures Frank was handing one at a time to Jon. Chen sent gifts of rare design and of special significance to Frank as the years passed, and Frank treasured them. They now belong to his children and family, and the letters of explanation Chen sent with them are still attached for anyone to read and enjoy.

Chapter Thirteen

Frank finally decided to tell Jon of the Spillman brothers. The claim was rich in some of the best ore they had ever seen. Three years they worked the mine during the summer months as soon as the snow melted to allow access into the mine. They used mules to carry the ore to the smelter and collect the rewards. There were thousands of dollars of raw profit for each year they spent at the mine.

The summer months were always spent up in the Colorado hills doing some form of mining. First in and near Central City and Black Hawk, then they ventured south to Lost Park and East Lost Park. In the winter, they lived in Denver in one of the boarding houses. In January of 1891, both men were clearly aware they were to change directions. In the last 2 weeks of April, the mine was prepped to be closed as they had planned. The mine entrance was disguised with the brown cement as they had decided and sealed on May 1, 1891. On May 2 early before dawn, they made their way out of East Lost Park into Lost Park for the last time. Howard French's map is in the possession of a Dalton relative who still lives in Lamar, Missouri—a block from the High School and a few short blocks from where President Harry S. Truman was born. It was the home of the Truman family where they lived before they moved to Grand View, Missouri.

Frank and Jon Dalton decided to close the mine and return to their homes in Lamar, Missouri. It was a strong desire each man felt within himself this must be done, and it must be done as soon as possible. It happened 18 months prior to the Sherman Silver Purchasing Act 1893. These inner premonitions were later considered by Frank and Jon to be divine intervention that moved the Dalton cousins to seal the mine entrance as they did. They had intended to return and open the mine in the future when the cost of silver was again at the price per ounce to produce silver and make a substantial profit.

They never returned to the mine together, and the exact location is only on the Spillman map. Unless you were to research the name "Louis Spillman" and find the original claim filed with the Park County township, now in the County Seat of the county. The Lost Park, East Lost Park area would be the closest verbal description of the location for the original mining claim. That is if Lou Spillman and his brother ever really filed a claim for their mine, and if you could find its specific location. The longitude and latitude would be so helpful, but that was something that was never considered until years later.

The decision to close the mine and sell all the real estate owned in Denver, Colorado, by late summer of 1891 was a strong desire of both men. The return to their hometown with the profits from sold business assets and the money from the gold dust was one of the best decisions the Dalton men ever made. They left Colorado return to Lamar, Missouri, with all they had accumulated from the hard work of the boarding houses, real estate, businesses, and most recently the final diggings from the East Lost Park mine.

With the upcoming economic disaster of the Colorado economy in 2 short years, they would read of this in the Missouri papers and thank the Good Lord for their exit 2 years prior. It was only then that they realized what a good and timely decision they had made. The Sherman Silver Purchasing Act in early 1893 changed forever the profitability of mining for silver in Colorado. This would eventually be a story Frank and Jon Dalton would tell with pride and a peaceful resolve for the rest of their lives.

So let's go back and pick up the story where we left off. The mine entrance was sealed May 1, 1891, using the rocks from the mine and colored concrete or cement made from a brown powdered clothes dye and sand from a nearby river bottom, "Good Ole Mother Earth," to give it a color more natural to the surrounding hillside. Frank had decided this would make the cement look natural and part of the rocky slope.

The two men had discussed this visit for quite a while before it was finalized. Their final and joint decision was to visit family in Lamar, Missouri, in the summer or early autumn of 1892.

This decision was just 6 months before the Dalton Gang robbed two banks simultaneously in Coffeeville, Kansas. That resulted in the death of every gang member except Bob Dalton who was tried, convicted, and sent to prison. The final and fatal days of the notorious Dalton Gang took place in October 1892.

Chapter Fourteen

Frank and Jon both later confessed each had a feeling as if they were encouraged by an invisible third partner to close and seal the Spillman mine and sell all the real estate property including the boarding houses and the many businesses, leave Colorado, and go home to Lamar, Missouri. After visiting family in Lamar, they planned to travel like Frank and his father had when they visited Washington, D.C., in Frank's early years. They wanted to take time and visit some of the historic cities and interesting places in these United States—places they had only read about. They wanted to stand on the very spots that were part of this country's great and historical past. Then they planned to return and establish in Missouri what they had done with businesses that were such a success in Colorado. It would be relatively easy to follow the same plan and process, just this time it would be in Lamar or another town in Missouri. "I like Kansas City," said Jon. "Its population is continuously growing, and it would offer the financial growth we need to see our businesses grow and prosper. A good part is that Kansas City is close enough we could take short trips to Lamar and visit family any time we want."

The banking plans and the business at hand was now an exit plan. They listed the boarding houses for sale. It was no time until prospective buyers were making offers and one by one the houses were sold for a good profit from the original price paid. The residential property had been converted into commercial income rental property. With the sale of each location, the proceeds from each sale were deposited in their local bank accounts.

The president of the Fifth National Bank of Denver, a Mr. William Wilson, and the Vice President, Mr. Peter Smyte, designed what they called a Security Carpetbag for travel with large amounts of money. The bank discouraged any individual from traveling with a large amount of cash money.

Mr. Smyte, the vice president of the bank, was originally a loan officer who had assisted Jon and Frank with many of their real estate purchases. Now a personal friend, he insisted the majority of the funds be sent by wire transfer to a bank in Independence, Missouri, where an account was set up in the names Jon James Robert Dalton and Franklin Randall Dalton. This was done with the funds accumulated from the real estate sales.

The money from the sale of the gold dust to the various smelters accumulated for the last few years was to be kept a secret. Jon and Frank decided to keep this information to themselves. These funds would travel with them in the special carpetbag. The bag was designed with a false bottom for bricks of five straps of bills placed side by side. A strap had 100 bills tightly held together by a band usually of paper with the denomination of the bills designated. A brick is five straps of 100 bills each, tightly banded together. The sides of the bag had individual sleeves that would accommodate and hold a number of straps upright in the false lining of the bag. Inside the bag on the side with the handle was a secret hidden compartment for important papers and documents. You could reach to the bottom of the bag and on the right side extend your fingers up and behind the lining and you could feel the security pouch, designed in the smooth flat area of the bag.

In the center of the bag, clothes or personal items could be placed to appear to be the only items in the bag.

Frank obtained the bag from the bank as a gift of appreciation to two loyal customers. He later packed the funds in the bag. Frank decided as an afterthought to place all the bank deposits and all the closing documents for the real estate sales in a safe place, and this pouch seemed to be just the ticket. He planned to later show Jon all the hidden features of the remarkable bag.

That evening Jon was amazed with the ingenious design of the Security Carpetbag. The hidden flap would hide and keep secure the confidential papers from the bank transactions. The special design of the bag and its contents were well hidden and unknown to anyone other than Frank and Jon. The local Denver company that manufactured the bag included a confidential agreement stating, "Our Security and Secrecies are only as good as yours. This product is only a design. You must utilize it with trust. Trust no one, and the product will keep and conceal your valuables safe and secure as you travel."

The money belts Jon had were of some use and a good thought, but the funds planned for travel were now secure in the carpetbag. Chen had made two suit jackets with long pockets in the special lining. Banker Pete Smyth set up special saving interest bearing investment accounts. The bank would later transfer the money from the sales of the real estate to any bank where Frank and Jon set up business accounts. The paperwork all signed and ready for the final transfer information was also in an envelope secure in the bag. The cousins were not planning on drawing any attention to themselves. No one would be the wiser that they were carrying any money, and it would all be concealed.

Their thoughts and future plans to buy the hotel building on Market Street with the gold dust mirrors would never come to pass. The hotel had three full stories, main floor dining room, meeting rooms, and ballroom. The second and third floors had spacious rooms to rent out to the general public. This was a wonderful dream and still brings a smile to the faces of the two men—just the very thought of it.

Plans were coming together to ride the train to Kansas City, Kansas, a ride to Kansas City, Missouri, and a planned appointment at a local bank in Independence, Missouri. Then it was on to visit St. Louis, Missouri, just to see the city, to walk the streets, and talk to locals and hear the many stories of the historic city. It was the original jumping off place in 1804 for the Louis and Clark expedition to find the Northwest passage to the Pacific and the eventual return in 1806. They wanted to walk the streets of St. Louis, the gateway to the west, one of the first frontier towns. Then back west with a stop in the town of Rolla, Missouri, to see an old friend Jon met a few years earlier. The young girl was traveling west with her aunt and uncle to visit Denver and met Jon on the train.

She soon decided to return home as the harsh winters of the Rockies had proven to be a bit much. She returned to her hometown, and eventually married an older local man who had owned the General Store and Mercantile for years in Rolla, Missouri. His wife had passed away; and after an appropriate time, he had married the younger woman. She had worked as a clerk, stocking shelves, and bookkeeper off and on in her growing up years.

Jon had originally met her on the train. She was always so very friendly and willing to befriend a young male traveler. She had probably written Jon as a lark using the address of Jon Dalton, General Delivery, Central City, Colorado, almost from the first month he had arrived. They had become pen pals you might say, with Jon receiving five letters to his one letter written in return.

Jon was lucky to compose two to three pages at most, which were usually sent out of shear guilt from the many he received from the Missouri acquaintance.

She wrote letters that were an in-depth divulging of every detail she experienced in her life, describing her every fantasy and intimate thought. Jon read every letter and each one was kept. Jon had learned so much just from reading the intricate aspects of being a woman. Such things as how she thought about herself, what a woman should do or not do for herself. Questions about men in general and why they do what they do. A young man in the city she had met and what had started out as simple friends had developed into a secret compromising situation that had since ended. What a wife could do when she was neglected by her husband. She had developed and devised ways of satisfying her inner hunger. Jon had no idea how to answer, so he would answer her question with a question.

Jon shared only the first few letters with Frank. Frank had considered traveling near or toward Jefferson City or Rolla, Missouri. Jon reluctantly admitted that she had mentioned on more than one occasion in her letters if Jon or his cousin Frank ever came through Rolla, her home was open. They had spare rooms that were never used. The Bruebaker Hotel, as she called her home, was far better than paying money for a few nights stay a local hotel.

She was now married and was very large and heavy, still willing to accommodate if only someone—anyone—would allow this hungry woman access to what would soon be an open mistake. The long hours it takes to operate a General Store was the work her husband had embraced for years. She would be a gracious hostess for the two men and attend to their every need for as long as they wanted to stay. Jon didn't want to go visit the woman, but Frank thought it would be a nice gesture and he thought Jon was being over reactionary in his comments about the young woman. "Why would you possibly be uncomfortable about a night or two in the home of a friend? We make it clear we have business in the area, thank them for their hospitality, and bid them farewell. We're out the door, on our way, off we go, lickety split down the road," said Frank.

Chapter Fifteen

The plan had been to stop at the bank in Jefferson City, Missouri, to open another bank account, then telegraph the Colorado bank and transfer funds. With business concluded, they would travel to Rolla, Missouri, to spend some time with Jon's old pen pal and exit in a hasty manner if needed. Then they would travel the most direct route straight south and home to Lamar, Missouri. Frank had decided to remove some of the money from the sides of the bag and have it lying loose ready for deposit inside the bag so as not to reveal even to the bank official who might be the bank president. The instructions "TRUST NO ONE" was a wise thing to always consider. A bank officer who would handle the large transaction could talk, and this secure bag design would eventually be known by anyone and eventually everyone.

Upon arrival at the bank that morning, there was a surprise for the Dalton cousins to see three armed men with bandanas covering their faces moving around inside the bank. "My, what in blue blazes are they doing?" said Frank, not believing his eyes. Frank and Jon had attempted to enter the bank and were standing just inside the doors. The men who were in the bank had finished taking as much money as they could and were making a hasty exit. They moved swiftly by Frank and Jon and were mounting their horses when shooting was heard outside. Some local men were shooting at the bank robbers as they were trying to flee the scene. The gang started to return fire.

Frank and Jon were standing at the doors when Frank lunged forward and grabbed Jon, and both men found themselves lying in the door of the bank. Frank had been shot and was slowly losing consciousness. This day had not started out well for the cousins. They were standing in the door of the bank as innocent bystanders. Now Frank was shot, wounded by a local man trying to stop the bank robbers. Jon was now kneeling by Frank yelling,

"Someone get a doctor! Frank has been shot! We have a wounded man here!"

Jon had dropped the carpetbag, and some of the money they had intended to deposit into the bank was lying out on the floor near the front doors of the bank. Jon was applying pressure to the wound on Frank's chest. He stayed with Frank and in no time the local doctor had arrived. Jon finally had asked for help to pick up the money and place it back in the bag. A bank employee came and helped replace the money and close the bag.

The doctor was a man with much experience in matters such as gunshot wounds. He made a quick initial examination to determine if the most apparent wound was his only wound. The doctor said, "We cannot move him until I get a stretcher and men to help move this man to my office. The bullet went clean through, but the exit wound is close to the spine; and it's impossible to know if any internal damage has been done."

"Who are you?" asked the Doctor. "I am Jon Dalton, a relative. I was with him when he was shot," said Jon.

"Stay here; I'll be right back. We can move him to my office. He will need some special care and attention. Keep pressure on the entry wound but don't press with much pressure on his back. I'll clean and bandage the wounds in my office. The bullet exit wound is close to the spine and we don't want to cause any damage." Jon waited with the carpetbag now close to his side, and then followed the Doctor and the two men carrying Frank on a stretcher to the Doctor's office.

Jon stayed with Frank until the Doctor told him, "We have done all we can. His body needs to heal and time will do the rest." Jon stayed for a while in the outer office; then as his mind cleared from the devastating experience, he went to tend to the horses still tied to the hitching post in front of the bank. He led the two animals to the local livery stable and paid for a full week's stay for care, feed and grain for the horses. Jon told the man at the livery that they might be there for a while. He briefly talked to the friendly man about all that had happened in the last hour and a half. He was told he could pay from week to week for as long as needed. Their saddles were placed in the tack room.

Jon left the livery with the saddlebags and the carpetbag and checked into a hotel near the doctor's office. He took a bath, changed his clothes, then returned to the doctor's office where he was told no change had been seen in Frank's condition. Jon attended the local Baptist Church and talked with the Pastor asking for prayer and shared Frank's unfortunate circumstances. The Pastor prayed with Jon and placed Frank on the church prayer list.

It was soon determined the notorious Dalton Gang had robbed the bank of an undetermined amount of money. They had made a clean get away. Some of the local men who had fired on the gang during their escape were sure they had put lead in the fleeing bandits. The local Sheriff had quickly organized a posse and made a hasty pursuit of the notorious "Wild Bunch," the Dalton Gang.

The bank employees, and specifically the bank manager, had noticed the large amount of cash money in the carpetbag. This information was passed along to the Sheriff Deputy Joe Caraway who was in charge of the investigation of the bank robbery. The Sheriff Al Wilkins was informed of this information upon his return from the failed attempt with the posse to catch the Dalton Gang. Who were these two strangers who had appeared at the same time the bank was being robbed with a large amount of cash in a suitcase? The fact that Frank Dalton was shot and in a state of coma from such a wound, his recovery uncertain, his chances slim at best. Jon had also remained in town and had even checked into a hotel raised specific interest to the Sheriff and his Deputy. It was now considered they were suspects and not just men who were in the wrong place at the wrong time. Jon was called into the Sheriff's office and questioned by Deputy Joe Caraway who decided he needed professional help and consulted with the District Attorney and was told to secure a deposition from Jon.

The Sheriff had been in the banking business prior to his career change into law enforcement. Sheriff Wilkins assisted the Deputy in organizing his investigation of the robbery and had made a great effort in questioning any and all witnesses including all bank employees. The initial part of his investigation was completed by late afternoon of the second day after the robbery. The town was settling back into the normal quiet life that had been so loudly interrupted with the bank robbery. This gave the town folk something to talk about and share their experiences of where they were and what they were doing during the robbery.

The witnesses although frozen in fear during the robbery were now self-declared heroes as the story was embellished each time it was told. It was the topic of almost every conversation for as many days as it could be kept alive, by asking, "Tell me again what you did or what really happened when you realized what was going on." A bank robbery was a tragic and monumental event for any bank employee who would hope it was a once in a lifetime experience.

However, in the course of time after Jon faced more questioning by Deputy Caraway, Jon was considered, if not a part of the original gang, he was an accomplice or Frank and Jon were lookouts for the Dalton gang. This large amount of money these two men were carrying must surely be stolen and made by ill gotten gain. With the same last name "Dalton" and the near to exact likeness in facial appearance to the men of the gang, determined by the local Deputy Sheriff from witnesses stating one of the men in the gang looks very much like Jon and the wounded man at the Doctor's office.

Jon was sitting in the office of the Doctor when Deputy Caraway and another man came and asked if he could accompany them to the Sheriff's office for some final questioning. As the three entered the Sheriff's office, Jon was told to sit in a chair by the wall. The Deputy and the second man with guns drawn told Jon he was being taken into custody and under arrest for suspicion of bank robbery. Jon was escorted to a cell and the door was closed and locked behind him. Jon was now residing in the local town jail. The Deputy insisted Sheriff Wilkins place an armed guard with a 24-hour schedule to watch Frank if he was to awaken and become violent or try to escape.

The shooting of Frank and Jon being arrested and locked in a jail cell was like walking into a strange nightmare, except it was in the full light of day. Frank was over with the local Doctor in a state of what the Doctor told Jon was a coma. The only possibility that had been uncovered through the criminal investigation assumed by Deputy Sheriff Joe Caraway was that Frank and Jon didn't walk into the bank as it was being robbed. They were part of the Dalton Gang and were guilty by name association being at the scene of the crime. The money in the carpetbag was money stolen from banks in other towns the gang had previously robbed.

It was assumed they were lookouts for the gang. The fact that Frank was shot and Jon remained was just part of bad luck and being caught. If they were just passing through, that now seems to be unlikely, said Deputy Sheriff Caraway. These men were both blood relatives of the notorious Dalton Gang. Jon openly and honestly confessed it to be true, never attempting to hide this fact from the first questioning. How blatant and brazen to remain in the very city and give a story as if they were innocent law-abiding citizens, when in fact, they were part of the original gang. The story spread to many of the citizens that Deputy Caraway and Sheriff Wilkins now had seen through the ruse and scam and was about to have justice served for the crimes committed. How could these men expect intelligent people to believe such a preposterous story?

With all the evidence coming forth as time passed, Sheriff Wilkins removed and searched through all of Jon's personal items from the hotel room. The now mysterious carpetbag of money was evidence and was placed in the bank vault of the very bank that was robbed days before. His intention was to connect this money to the bank robbery or most likely stolen from other banks that had been robbed in the Kansas territory. He was sure now from the intense investigation conducted by Deputy Caraway of fact and more than just suspicion. His consideration was if Jon and Frank were not guilty of this robbery, they are guilty of other bank robberies with stolen money found in their possession.

The Deputy Sheriff, in an attempt to substantiate the guilt of these two men, had the local printer make up posters with Frank's and Jon's facial appearance and their physical description sent to Sheriffs' offices throughout Kansas where local banks had been robbed in the past few months. The attempt was to see if bank employees could recognize these men from the posters to connect them with any other bank robberies in the Kansas territory.

Chapter Sixteen

The Honorable Judge Leonard Monteleone was summoned from the county seat. He arrived in town and made what seemed to be unusual haste to set a trial date for the following Monday. The Judge assigned a young lawyer to represent Jon Dalton. Frank, still incapacitated and in a coma, would be tried by a court of law when and if he became conscious and physically healthy enough to stand trial.

The young defense attorney filed for a continuance for the trial date to have additional time to prepare for the trial. This would allow the attorney and Jon time to pursue and develop a proper defense. The continuance was denied. The ruling for the original court date remained—the right to a fair and speedy trial would not be deterred.

Jon asked Sheriff Wilkins for a Bible and was truly thankful for the Bible Sheriff Wilkins gave him. Jon saw personal notes in places in the Bible, and he thought this might have been Wilkins' personal Bible. He told Jon to keep the Bible, "Kid, you keep it, you really need it. It's yours to keep."

Jon read and spent time in prayer. He wrote a letter to his family trying to explain what has happened to him and Frank and the possible negative outcome. "We might never be coming home," he sadly confessed in the closing remarks of his letter. Although written, it was never mailed. One of the deputies placed it in the bottom drawer of the big desk in the outer office of the jail. It was never determined if this was a mishap or intentional.

Jon spent most of the time in his cell reading the Bible and praying. He confessed, "I have been working in Colorado for years. I was striving with all that was within me to get wealthy. I gave place to everything apart from my faith in the Lord Jesus Christ. Now, I can't go to church, or ask the preacher or church to agree with me in prayer. The Lord Jesus Christ will be my advocate and represent me and deliver me and heal Frank."

"The Bible is the inspired 'Word of God,' a very powerful book. I pray and ask God to heal Frank of something I really do not understand and awaken my cousin from this coma. I will be taken to court and tried for crimes I say I did not do and no one is listening. I feel alone and no one is hearing or trying to believe what I am saying. *I will not say or confess it aloud, but I feel as if there is no hope for my life, as I have known it. I will believe and confess the Word wherein I place all my hope.* I will only confess the Word of God and not speak one negative word against what I have prayed, confessed, and believe. I will not condemn myself with negative words from my mouth."

Monday is only 3 days away, and no telegraph has arrived from Colorado. The young and inexperienced lawyer sent the telegraph but did no follow up after no response from the Colorado bank. Mr. William E. Wilson, the bank president, was away from the bank on personal business so the telegram was signed for by a new employee, a replacement secretary. Not knowing exactly what to do, she placed the envelope in the IN basket on the president's desk with the assumption this was just another telegram for Mr. Wilson. The telegram was supposed to be marked URGENT, but that had failed to happen.

Mr. Wilson had actually taken a few days off to enjoy some fly-fishing for trout in the Colorado Rockies. His vacation location was unknown, and he will be informed of the request upon his return. Mr. Peter Smyte, the Vice President, is now in charge of all banking business, but the telegram was shuffled deeper in the basket and assumed to be of no important business significance.

A local schoolteacher was asked by Deputy Caraway to assist the young attorney. Her services were needed to write out a deposition of the most recent past of Jon and Frank Dalton and how they had happened to be at the bank on the morning in question, with detail of how and why such a large amount of funds was in the possession of the two accused men. The Deputy believed this would lead to further incriminating evidence of the two men and link them to the Dalton Gang and the crime.

The schoolteacher was not selected at random. She was to assist the Deputy Sheriff, but an ulterior motive was also a consideration. The Deputy would be forced to spend time with this young woman, and get to know her in a more personal way. The young lady was a possible candidate for the as of yet unfilled position of the future Mrs. Joe Caraway.

Miss Susan Frost was very meticulous and detailed in writing out the words of the deposition. This was something almost anyone who could read and write could have done. Working and writing as a scribe for the Deputy Sheriff and the District Attorney in the Courthouse was not her idea of something she really wanted to do.

Jon was reading aloud Psalms 120 through 123, praying aloud, and placing his trust and hope for divine intervention. His hand was placed on these verses claiming God's promises for deliverance from the great trouble he is in. The Infallible Word of God—the God-breathed book the BIBLE, prayer, and fasting were Jon's only hope. Jon was now trusting Jesus for deliverance like no other time in his young life. Jon's contrite prayer was for the supernatural hand of protection and deliverance by God from their dire circumstances. God must intervene before it is too late.

Susan made a decision after hearing Jon present his statement and all the related circumstances of his and Frank's lives and experiences in Colorado for the last few years. Jon's forthright honesty in answering the questions he had answered repeatedly with the same precise answers gave pause to the school teacher. This man was in fact telling the truth. The final draft was completed and presented to the Deputy, the District Attorney, and Jon's attorney.

As Susan reread the lengthy copy of the sworn statement, she felt a certainty within herself that this man was telling the truth and he could be innocent. Susan Frost, now the unofficial assistant to the Sheriff, was increasingly interested in this man and his life threatening circumstances. She was only the scribe for the final deposition. She now had the complete story, and she saw some of the confusion and discrepancies that needed to be verified and confirmed. Susan told the Sheriff that he needed to check this connection with the Denver bank and verify this information.

The Sheriff said, "This is not something we need to follow up on for these men. They were in the bank, and upon their exiting with the bank robbers, their horses were also tied outside of the bank. Then there is the matter of the large carpetbag full of money they were carrying. No one carries that much money in a carpetbag."

"Jon Dalton told you in his deposition about the money and the sales of real estate," said Susan.

"The defendant's attorney has already sent a telegraph and is awaiting confirmation from the Colorado bank as we speak. I worked in a bank, and they are very professional and follow procedures with these matters, trust me. I worked in a bank, and I trust the banking industry," said Sheriff Wilkins.

The Baptist Church was praying for Frank and Jon due to the insistence of Miss

Susan Frost. "I know these men are innocent. I believe we will be disobedient if we hesitate and do not pray for the Lord Jesus Christ to be the Lord of their defense."

The court trial was all new to Jon. He had no prior experience with the legal system and the serious matters he was facing. He received a crash course with Susan as she spent the evenings educating herself and Jon with all aspects of criminal law.

The District Attorney had questioned each and every one of the town's people who was a witness of any type or thought they needed to be a witness. Some were hoping for their 15 minutes as a celebrity and go on record as part of this historic trial.

Chapter Seventeen

I t was late in the afternoon 2 days before the trial was to start. Susan was sitting as usual in a wooden chair outside the cell. Jon was sitting inside on the bed along the far wall. The unlikely duo this day found themselves lost in conversation with questions of their lives and past experiences. They spent over an hour talking and laughing about things in their lives—some parallel, some were varied and of no close connection at all. Jon had told Susan he was grateful for her prayers and the prayers of the Baptist Church for him and Frank.

Susan told Jon, "Well, I have not always been a Baptist. I was born into a family that had been of the Catholic faith for many generations." Seeing a look of interest on

Jon's face, Susan continued. "My father, who I dearly love and respect, is one of the people who is not pleased with my change of faith to put my assurance in Jesus Christ alone and to become a member of the Baptist Church. I had a good friend, and we would walk and talk together on a mountain near where I was living. We talked of many things, but as we walked we were talking about the teaching of the Bible. He was a protestant believer, a Baptist, and I was of course a Catholic. We talked about the things of God many times as we would walk. I enjoyed just being outside to feel the cool breeze on my skin and smell the clean fresh air, the warmth of the sun, which could get rather hot as we walked. His desire was for me to place my faith and trust in the Lord Jesus Christ for salvation. He wanted me to be saved, be born again as he called it."

"One day when we were hiking and talking, this young man said, 'You already know what the Bible teaches about these things. You just need to decide that you believe them.' As we continued to walk, I thought to myself, 'I do believe what the Bible says. I have heard it for most of my life.' I purposed in my heart I believe the Bible is God's Word. I believe with my heart Jesus Christ is the Son of God. I believe he died and was raised from the dead for us all. As we hiked along something changed in me. I was never the same after that. I knew that I believed what the Bible says, what it teaches. It was like a knowing, a new awareness and I could tell there was a difference."

"The two of us attended a church service some time after that. At the end of the message, they gave an opportunity to pray aloud and confess Jesus Christ as Lord and Savior. I prayed a prayer that day, and I was born again. Romans 10:9-10, 'That if thou shalt confess with thy mouth the Lord Jesus, and shalt believe in thine heart that God hath raised him from the dead, thou shalt be saved. For with the heart man believeth unto righteousness; and with the mouth confession is made unto salvation.'"

"I was reading my Bible, and I had some questions. The Priest in our local parish was very open to answer my questions. It seemed to me his answers were memorized. He spoke as if he were reciting a dialogue. I decided to go to another Priest, and he gave almost the same answers to the same questions. The Catholic Church has taught these teachings and beliefs for faith and practice for centuries. The church states any teaching it has accepted takes supremacy over the Bible. The Catholic Church has the first and the final word, period, no question. Papal law is final. It was something the priests were taught and memorized from their seminary or ministerial teaching. The priest taught this to the people of the church, so it must be from God. It must be correct; who would ever question the word proclaimed for faith and practice of the largest church on the earth."

"I started reading the Bible on my own and this is what I found in reading the Bible. At the time of the crucifixion of Christ, the veil of the temple was rent or torn from the top to the bottom. Let me read it to you from my Bible," said Susan.

"You carry a Bible with you?" asked Jon.

"It's in my bag with the books I brought; but yes, Jon, I do carry a Bible with me. I read it every morning. I have a motto, 'No Bible—No Breakfast.' I read it every day; I read it aloud. I try to memorize specific Bible verses that are needed to understand what the Spirit of God wants us all to believe in our hearts. It's one thing to memorize the word, but quite another to have it in your heart."

Susan said, "Some people miss God by about 18 inches. How is that, you might ask? Well, they read the Bible and have an intellectual understanding, a mental assent, or head knowledge. It is important to believe within yourself, in your heart; to say mentally aloud, 'I believe what the Bible says. It's God's word—the first and final authority.' 'So then faith cometh by hearing, and hearing by the Word of God.,' Romans 10:17 'For with the heart, man believeth unto righteousness; and with the mouth, confession is made unto salvation,' Romans 10:10."

"This is what I understand the scripture teaches and now believe; the veil in the temple being torn from the top to the bottom gives us access to God. Matthew 27:50-51, 'Jesus, when he had cried again with a loud voice, yielded up the Ghost. And, behold, the veil of the temple was rent in twain from the top to the bottom; and the earth did quake and the rocks rent.' I have come to believe through study that the veil of its weave and thickness was impossible for a man to tear specifically from the top to the bottom. This tearing of the veil I believe was an act of God that gives us direct access to Father God."

"These verses make it clear Jesus is our high priest and our advocate with the Father. Ephesians 2:8-9, 'For by grace are you saved through faith; and not of your selves: it is a gift of God: Not of works, lest any man should boast.' Ephesians 2:13, 14 and 18, 'But now in Christ Jesus ye who were sometimes far off are made nigh by the blood of Jesus. For he is our peace, who hath made both one, and hath broken down the middle wall of partition between us. For through him we both have access by one Spirit unto the Father.' We can go directly to the Father God with Jesus Christ and our intermediary, go-between, or our mediator. I Timothy 2:5, 'There is one mediator between God and man, the man Christ Jesus.' Hebrews 4:14-16, "Seeing then that we have a great high priest, that is passed into the heavens, Jesus the Son of God, let us hold fast our profession. For we have not an high priest which cannot be touched with the feelings of our infirmities; but was in all points tempted like as we are, yet without sin. Let us therefore come boldly unto the throne of grace, that we may obtain mercy, and find grace to help in time of need.' Let me read Hebrews 9:15, 'And for this cause he is the mediator of the new testament, that by means of death, for the redemption of the transgressions that were under the first testament, they which are called might receive the promise of eternal inheritance.'"

"We have access to God the Father through Jesus Christ our Lord. Let's read Hebrews 10:10-17, 'By the which we are all sanctified through the offering of the body of Jesus Christ once for all. And every priest standeth daily ministering and offering the same sacrifices, which can never take away sin. But this man, after he had offered one sacrifice for sin forever, sat down on the right hand of God. From henceforth expecting till his enemies become his footstool. For by one offering he hath perfected forever them that are sanctified. Whereof the Holy Ghost also is a witness to us; for after that he had said before, This is the covenant I will make with them after those days, saith the Lord, I will put my laws into their hearts, and in their minds I will write them; And their sins and iniquities will I remember no more.'"

"In reading this passage, it clearly states children are to confess our sins to the father. I John 2:1-2, 'My little children, these things write I unto you that you sin not. And if any man sin, we have an advocate with the Father, Jesus Christ the Righteous.' I looked up the word Advocate. It means supporter, benefactor, aficionado or a devotee."

Susan smiled, giggled slightly, and with a twinkle in her eyes she said "Simply put, Jon, one who is the representative for us, our advocate Jesus Christ, God's Son the Righteous became the payment for the original sin of Adam and for every sin for all mankind. We confess our sins to Jesus the only begotten Son of God who became the sacrificial Lamb, the offering for sin. Jesus Christ is our advocate placing his life and death as a sacrifice for our life and our sin. Jesus Christ died in our place. He took our sin and condemnation, and we receive eternal life and his righteousness."

"Now, Jon, listen as I read I John 2:2 'And he is the propitiation for our sins; and not for ours only, but also for the sins of the whole world.' Propitiation means atoning sacrifice. Atonement is covering with the blood of Christ. God looks through this blood covering atonement and sees holiness instead of sin. Is that good? That makes it very simple and understandable for me anyway," said Susan.

"Let me read from the Old Testament Isaiah 53:5, 'But he was wounded for our transgressions, he was bruised for our iniquities: the chastisement of our peace was upon him; and with his stripes we are healed.' I am a schoolteacher. I assign every student of the Bible, every believer, the assignment to read and memorize this passage. Isaiah 53:1-12 was prophetically recorded in the Bible hundreds of years before Christ was born, lived, and died for the sins of all mankind. It is here foretold and documented for all to read. It's God's plan of salvation and redemption for all mankind if they choose to believe, accept and receive it."

I also think this is presented clearly in John 10:1-5. Let's read it together. 'Verily, verily, I say unto you, He that entereth not by the door into the sheepfold, but climbeth up some other way, the same is a thief and a robber. But he that entereth by the door is the shepherd of the sheep. To him the porter openeth; and the sheep hear his voice; and he calleth his own sheep by name, and leadeth them out. And when he putteth forth his own sheep, he goeth before them, and the sheep follow him; for they know his voice. And a stranger will they not follow, but will flee from him; for they know not the voice of the stranger.' The sheep know the voice of the shepherd and the voice of the stranger they will not follow. So if we listen to a priest and confess our sins to a priest who gives us penance for our sins that Jesus Christ paid the debt Jesus being the Atoning Sacrifice."

"Read with me, I John 1:9, 'If we confess our sins, he is faithful and just to forgive us our sins, and to cleanse us from all unrighteousness.' If we confess our sins to the Father in Jesus name, all our sins are forgiven. Jesus already paid the price. The Priest supposedly passes on the forgiveness of God to the believer then tells us to pray, say, and do something additional this is not what the Bible teaches. Are we not listening to a stranger's voice?" said Susan.

"As I grew up in the Catholic Church, another teaching I was taught was praying to Mary the mother of Jesus, praying to Saint Christopher, praying to St. Francis of Assisi, praying to the statutes in the church of St Genevieve. Catholics are to pray to the saints and statues so they will intercede for man. The word intercede means to intervene, to plead, to ask on someone's behalf. I Thessalonians 1:9b, 'and how ye turned to God from idols, to serve the living and true God.' I John 5:21, 'Little children, keep yourselves from idols, amen.'"

"I will now present scriptural proof, God the Father is watching over us and he intercedes for us. Jesus intercedes for us, and the Holy Spirit intercedes for us. Our Heavenly Father has committed himself to our protection. Deuteronomy 32:11-12. 'As the eagle stirreth up her nest, fluttering over her young, spreadeth broad her wings, taketh them, bearing them on her wings; So the Lord alone did lead him, and there was no strange God with him.' Isaiah 59:16, 'And he saw that there was no man, and wondered that there was no intercessor; therefore his arm brought salvation unto him; and his righteousness, it sustained him.' Colossians 2:13-14, 'And you, being dead in your sins and the uncircumcision of your flesh, hath he quickened together with him, having forgiven you all trespasses. Blotting out the handwriting of ordinances that was against us, which was contrary to us, and took it out of the way, nailing it to the cross.' This is very GOOD, listen to this," said Susan. "John 5:44, 'How can you believe, which receive honor one of another, and seek not the honor that cometh from God only.'"

"Jesus is in heaven praying for you also. Romans 8:34, 'Who is he that condemneth? It is Christ that died, yea rather, that is risen again, who is even at the right hand of God, who also maketh intercession for us.' Hebrews 9:14, 'How much more shall the blood of Christ, who through the eternal Spirit offered himself without spot to God, purge your conscience from dead works to serve the living God?' Jon, look this up; read it with me. Hebrews

7:25, 'Wherefore he is able to save them to the uttermost that come unto God by him, seeing he ever liveth to make intercession for them.' The uttermost, 'He is able to save them to the uttermost that come to God, by him.'"

"The Holy Spirit is on the earth interceding for you continuously to the Father. Romans 8:27, 'He maketh intercession for the saints according to the will of God.' I Peter 1:2, 'Elect according to the foreknowledge according to God the Father, through sanctification of the Spirit, unto obedience and sprinkling of the blood of Jesus Christ; grace unto you, and peace be multiplied.' We the children of God cannot imagine the magnitude or the greatness of God's desires for us. This is why our prayers are often ineffective, incomplete, and go unanswered. We need to pray the Word of God and place God's word in our prayers while we form the words we pray. I Corinthians 2:9, 'Eye hath not seen, or ear heard, neither have entered into the heart of man, the things which God has prepared for them that love him.'"

"Mary the mother of Jesus was most blessed among women and she was like no other. She was a blessed virgin and a woman after God's own heart as was David a man after God's own heart. She was a believer of Jesus and would not desire anyone to place her above her Lord and Savior. She saw Jesus on the cross, the empty tomb, again after some 40 days before he ascended into heaven, and she was a part of the New Testament church. Acts 1:1-9, 'Among those present were the eleven apostles. These all continued with one accord in prayer and supplication, with the women, and Mary the mother of Jesus, and with his brethren.' Mary the mother of Jesus was one of the people who witnessed Jesus when he spoke to them before his ascension up in to heaven.'"

"Acts 1:13-14, Mary the mother of Jesus was also present in the upper room as one of the hundred and twenty who were waiting and praying. She was one of those who the Holy Ghost came upon with cloven tongues of fire. She was a blessed woman. She never says or does anything that would draw attention to herself and away from the Lord Jesus Christ. At the marriage supper in Cana, John 2:3-5, 'and when they wanted wine, the mother of Jesus saith unto him, they have no wine. Jesus saith unto her, Woman what have I to do with thee? Mine hour is not yet come. His mother saith unto the servants, Whatsoever he saith unto you do it.'"

Mary's cousins Zacharias and Elizabeth had a son named John, who became John the Baptist. An angel appeared to Zacharias and told of the birth of his son who was to be called John, and he shall be filled with the Holy Ghost from his mother's womb. Mary the mother of Jesus was also a cousin to John the Baptist. John said, 'I indeed baptize you with water unto repentance, but he that cometh after me is mightier than I, whose shoes I am not worthy to bear; he shall baptize with the Holy Ghost and with fire,' Matthew 3:11. John also said of Jesus, 'He must increase, but I must decease,' John 3:30."

Chapter Eighteen

"Susan, I have never had anyone take so much time with me to share the things you have. From you I have learned so much," said Jon.

"Jon, you are just motivated because of the problems of life and the possibility of what may happen in the upcoming trial and what might be its outcome. I am a teacher, and you are an adept pupil. Many who teach in areas of higher learning will have one pupil who is more eager than all the rest, and the teacher teaches to that one pupil. When in reality, all of the students learn and benefit from the presentation of the subject matter—some more than others," said Susan.

"One important thing we all need to realize is no one person knows everything about all aspects of life. You surely have heard a famous quote, 'The jack of all trades, the master of none.' This quote could have meant far more if it were to be, 'The jack of all trades, but the Master of one.' The truth we should glean from this statement is ultimately each one of us should have one specific trade as your area of expertise, area of ability, and craftsmanship. Paul said in the Bible, 'I press toward the mark for the prize of the high calling of God in Christ Jesus,' Philippians 3:14."

"The Golden Rule in the Word of God says, 'And as you would that men should do unto you, do ye also to them likewise,' Luke 6:31. Simply put, Jon; 'Do unto others as you would have others do unto you.' We all have our life experiences, and we have learned from parents, relatives, teachers, and other mentors if we chose to listen and heed what they were saying."

"The experience you find yourself in today can be a learning experience and you can benefit from the lessons learned. That is, if you to choose to. You surely have heard some people say, 'Bad things always happen to me,' 'It's one bad thing happening to me after another,' 'If it wasn't for bad luck, I wouldn't have any luck at all.' Strike these comments from your mouth, and never say anything like that again. Read Matthew 21:21, 'Jesus answered and said unto them, Verily I say unto you, if you have faith, and doubt not, ye shall not only do this which is done unto the fig tree, but also if ye shall say unto this mountain, be thou removed, and be thou cast into the sea; it shall be done.'"

"One of my favorite verses is Mark 11:23b, 'But shall believe that those things which he saith shall come to pass; he shall have whatsoever he saith.' The Bible teaches 'from the abundance of the heart the mouth speaketh.' Do not speak words against what you pray. Do not say things you do not want to manifest in your life," said Susan.

"Where is that verse found in the Bible?" asked Jon.

"I don't exactly know. Why don't you look it up. I think it is Matthew 12:34," said Susan.

"Our first mentors are mother, father, grandparents, and other family members. Most all relatives will teach us if we take the time to listen to what they are saying. Some don't teach; you must watch and learn. The school is often the first introduction of a teacher, a mentor outside of the family. The American Indians used oral tradition to teach every child all they needed to know of life, family, and the rules of the people of the tribe. The life teaching was as varied as the different peoples and tribes from all across North America," said Susan.

Jon was looking at Susan and listening to every word she was saying. When she stopped talking, Jon looked down and to the left as he brought up his line of vision looking directly into Susan's eyes. He said, "I want to thank you for all you have done. You have taken so much time, and I am so grateful."

Susan said "Jon, Jon." She waited until his eyes met hers, and she said, "Teaching and helping others to learn what they most need to know is what I do. You, sir, are the first, the first adult male apart from the male students I have spent time with who had no idea what it was they needed to know. Any man who listens to a woman might find a wealth of knowledge if he takes the time to listen."

"This could be a divine appointment set up by God the Father for you, Jon. Why? Because I am skilled in finding answers and solving problems, then presenting what I have learned to another so they can understand and use the information to hopefully learn so they can solve the problems in their lives. What you need to realize is we both have learned what is involved with the law, not just concerning your upcoming trial, but how the legal system works and the procedures that will be followed and why."

"I have a question for you, Mr. Jon Dalton., If you died today, would you go to heaven?"

Jon sat and stared at Susan for a long moment and finally said, "Yes, I would go to heaven if I died. I have received the Lord Jesus as my Lord and Savior." Lowering his eyes, he exhaled a long breath, and said, "I must confess I have allowed other things to take first place in my daily life. To my credit, since I was arrested for bank robbery, I have read the Bible and prayed more at any one time than ever before. I have allowed the daily demands of life to keep me from what was really important. I have yielded to all the demands of life and become too busy to do what is the first priority of my life—Bible reading and prayer. Yes, Jesus is my Savior, but he is not the Lord of my life. I know I must give him first place," said Jon.

"I believe there are times in our lives when God uses experiences in our life to get our attention: to end one season and start another, or to clarify a life assignment that God has for us; to close one door and open another, to end one part of your life and open a new level of service; an occasion for us to be blessed of the Father God and Jesus Christ," said Susan.

"You, Jon, seem to be at one of those times; here today you find yourself in one of those places. I believe we must pray about the dire possibilities you are facing. I will pray for you first. I feel you need to pray aloud for yourself, asking all you believe you need and desire God to do to intervene on your behalf. I will pray again after you pray in a prayer of agreement with you. I believe the prayer of agreement is very important and is necessary for you in what you are facing.

Jon knelt on his knees inside the jail cell. Susan knelt on her knees by her chair. Susan extended her hands through the bars. Jon hesitated, and then took her hands. Susan prayed. Jon then prayed, wept, and prayed again. When he was through, he said, "Amen."

Susan said, "I will pray a prayer of agreement with you, Father God in Jesus name, I, Susana Marie Frost, Susan Mary Frost, now pray in agreement with Jon Dalton. We claim Matthew 18:20, 'For where two or three are gathered together in my name, there am I in the midst of them.' We also agree with the Lord God almighty in Deuteronomy 32:30, 'How should one chase a thousand, and two put ten thousand to flight, except their Rock had sold them, and the Lord hath shut them up?' Joshua 23:10, 'One man of you shall chase a thousand; for the Lord your God, he it is that fighteth for you, as he hath promised you.' In Jesus name I pray, Amen, amen." Susan then added, "As it has been said, so let it be done."

She looked up and said, "My mother is Spanish, and my father is English. Therefore, I have two separate pronunciations of my name."

Jon slowly released Susan's hands, stood to his feet, turned and walked slowly back across the cell as Susan sat again on the chair and looked directly at him. She parsed her lips, looked down and smoothed her dress, pushing her hands forward to her knees and then back to her lap. She moved her hands down the sides of her dress as if to smooth and straighten it, then gently ever so slightly lifting the material with her thumbs and fore fingers. Upon releasing the dress material, it fell from the middle of the black high top shoes she was wearing until only the toes of her shoes could be seen from the hem of her dress. Then clasping her hands, she placed them in her lap. Lifting her shoulders, she took a deep and long breath and exhaled slowly, looking at Jon with a wide smile and said, "It's done. We have done all we can to ask for God's help and deliverance for you in this matter, Jon. The victory is ours—the best outcome. Now rest in God the Father, Jesus Christ the Son, and the Holy Ghost—my very best friend."

Chapter Nineteen

In the courtroom as the days passed, it looked grim from the beginning; and the fear of fears of Jon and Susan were confirmed. On the day that appeared to be the final day of the trial, the Judge was handed the final decision of the Jury.

The telegraph agent who was hard pressed to stay in the telegraph office and teach his young nephew how to send and receive telegraph messages, received a very important, long-awaited message. He told the boy to run to the courthouse to fetch Miss Susan Frost. Tell her I have the telegram for her, and she needs to come and sign for it. Upon receiving the news of the telegraph, Susan left the courthouse and went to the telegraph office to sign for the telegram.

The Judge stated Jon Dalton has been found to be guilty of bank robbery. The Honorable Judge Leonard Monteleone had made the final verdict known from the jury to the court and everyone in the room and outside the Court House.

When Jon's sentence was presented and he was found guilty with the Judge reading the verdict, a rebellious faction of local town men started the preplanned lynch mob that would send out a strong message to every bank robber everywhere. Some local men grabbed the Sheriff and his Deputy's guns and tied their hands and feet and took them from the courtroom to the jail where they were locked into a cell with one man to guard them. One man who was working as a deputy and had been guarding Frank Dalton at the Doctor's office was taken by gunpoint, walked to the jail, and placed into one the of the locked cells.

Jon was taken from the courtroom out into the street. Some man tied Jon's hands together, and two others placed him on the back of a horse. A rope had been thrown over the large branch of a tree and placed around Jon's neck.

With the telegram in her hand, Susan sprinted with all her might up the hard packed dirt of the main street. Susan ran up the street yelling, "This cannot happen. You are trying to hang an innocent man." She was hit in the chest by a flying elbow from someone in the large crowd that poured out of the Court House. Susan, with the wind knocked out of her, struggled to her feet. A second attempt by Susan was stopped as she was hit in the face—her nose started to bleed. While sitting on the hard dirt of the street, something stirred in the young woman, and she started to get angry.

Susan stood up to her feet and grabbed the pistol from the holster of a man standing next to her. She ran through the crowd and stood in front of the horse and grabbed hold of the horse's reins. She then yells, "STOP! STOP right now, you Gaul Damn Sons ah Bitches! I will shoot any man who moves toward me. Ned Bentley, the bank president, where are you? I know you are here today."

"I am over here," a small and shallow voice is heard in the back of the crowd.

"Go to the bank and remove the carpetbag, and bring it out here. You will soon understand why I need you to do this, Ned. Please, take time to hear me out!" The crowd was as obedient as scolded school children. They stood still and only a few muffled words were heard in the near silence.

The banker finally appeared on the street, and Susan yelled to him. "You open the carpetbag and reach down the side and you will feel the edge of a flap. Move your fingers to the edge, and you will be able to pull the material away from the outside of the bag. Pull it out and slip your hand behind the material. There are papers behind the flap. Take them out and read them. She looked at Jon and nodded her head. "Do you remember?"

"Yes, I do. That's exactly right; those papers . . . ," said Jon, his voice trailed off as fear started to subside and hope was felt to start to rise up from deep within.

A man lunged forward, and Susan fired. The bullet ripped through his upper arm. With sheer exhilaration of the moment, the man spun and fell to the ground. Susan quickly calmed the horse, "Whoa, whoa, steady, easy, whoa, whoa." A long moment passed as every eye was now on the school teacher. "I said, I mean business; no one is going to be hung here today for a crime I know Jon Dalton didn't commit." She cocked the hammer back on the revolver. "I will kill the next man who moves toward me." She held the horse's reins and said again "Whoa, whoa, now it's ok, stand, stand easy now, easy," she said to calm the horse.

The banker yelled, "I found them and listen to this, these papers are deposits for a large amount of money, more than what is in this satchel. I have real estate loan closing papers for numerous properties signed and dated just a few weeks ago by Jon and Frank Dalton. I have many signed and dated banking papers, a savings account ledger, and investment accounts. The Sheriff had asked me to count the money before we placed it in the bank vault as evidence. I am sorry, Jon, I realize I was wrong for what I testified in court. These papers confirm this money is all legitimate business funds, the dates place you in Colorado for at least 3 years," said the banker.

"Ned Bentley, come here and read this telegram from the president of the bank in Colorado." Susan said, "If these men are telling the truth about the money they are carrying with them and these bank papers have dates for the last three years, I say they are telling the truth about being businessmen from Colorado and just happen to have the name 'Dalton.' If their names were Higgins, Bentley, or Smith, they would not have ever been facing bank robbery charges here today."

The banker said, "Susan is right. These papers confirm they came by this money legally through business. This telegram is legal confirmation for Jon and Frank Dalton with account holdings in excess of these funds in the Colorado bank. I would stake my banking career on it," said the banker. "They are more than legitimate businessmen, and just happen to have entered the bank during the robbery and have the same last name as the Dalton Gang."

"Judge, this evidence should clear these men of all the charges, right?" said Susan. Her dress was a mess from the bleeding from her nose which was dripping on the front of her dress making an ever growing red blotch.

The Judge said, "Bentley, bring those papers to me, would you please." It was just over a full minute when the Judge said, "In respect to the most recent evidence presented here today from the Denver banking documents, this telegram, Mr. Bentley's professional recommendation, and the argument presented by the unofficial Clerk of the Court, Miss Susan Frost, I declare Jon Dalton not guilty of the charges of bank robbery. Get him down at once," said the Judge.

"Someone get the Sheriff. You men there, Lip-shits, Slab-field, and Oliver Shag-nasty, you were the chief instigators of this lynch mob. Where is the Sheriff anyway? What have you men done with him and the Deputy? Where is Sheriff Wilkins?" asked the Judge.

"We tied him up. He's in the jail with the deputies," said Lip-shits. The Judge said, "You men, all of you, go to the jail and release the Sheriff and his Deputies, then come to the courthouse. I will show some leniency if you bring the Sheriff safely with you. Bentley, you go with them and tell the Sheriff about the banking papers, and make sure the Sheriff is informed of all that happened in the last few minutes.

"I said, someone get Mr. Jon Dalton down and free his hands, and do it right now."

"You, Sir, have my apologies. You are free to go. I would say you have the right to counter sue this town and the County for damages. You come see me, and I will personally inform you of your rights if you so desire. There was almost a gross miscarriage of justice here today, almost a reproach on my career, and most of all this town and a lynch mob would have hung an innocent man.

The Judge said "Miss Frost, you young lady, could be arrested for discharging a firearm in the city limits, and you acted falsely in communications to a Colorado bank as a Clerk of the County Court."

"I was also most recently informed of that bit of information," the District Attorney was smiling and looking around shaking his head.

"However, due to the extenuating circumstances, both charges are hereby dropped. You might take note, missy, you have acted very ruthless and unethical here today," said the Judge.

Someone said, "Judge, Judge, give her a break, let it rest."

"Who, who said that? I heard that," said the Judge." He finally smiled, and with a mocking hand wave, he turned and walked toward the Court House.

Jon took Susan in his arms and hugged her. Blood from her nose was now smeared on his cheek and on the front of his shirt. Someone walked by Susan and handed her a handkerchief, and she held it to her nose.

Chapter Twenty

The man Susan had shot was already at the Doc's office and had received a small glass of liquid for his pain. He was told not to drink any whiskey while he was treated for his arm, which was bandaged and taped as he was laying on his back on the examining table.

The deputy said with a big smile, "You do have the right to press charges against Miss Susan Frost for shooting you, ya know."

"I'll be danged if I will. I was shot cleaning my pistol out at the ranch. I don't want the world to know I was pistol shot by a school teacher, a female yelling and cussing, a pistol tottin hussy in love with some Colorado boy named Jon Dalton. You keep your mouth shut, Doc, or I will, I'll . . . ."

"Ya darn fool, the whole town saw you get shot. How you gonna keep that quiet?" said Doc. "Everyone in the whole county was there and saw ya get shot."

"Well, I guess you're right. I don't know, I just feel something awful. I need another drink, and I will have to think on it," said Ray Stevens.

"You better not drink any whiskey while I am treating you with Laudanum," said Doc.

"I think you do need another drink, and I might just be hard pressed to join ya," said Doc laughing and pointing at Ray. "For the pure embarrassment you have caused yourself here today, Ray," said Doc. "So you think the school teacher is in love with that Dalton boy?"

"Why heck yes, I do. Any woman would do what she did—she was just protecting her man. It's natural bred instinct in some of them women folk. They make up their mind, and they are hell bent to do what they have to do. I have seen a woman trail a man all the way cross the country from Kansas City, Missouri, out and eventually up into the mountains to Buena Vista, Colorado," said

Ray Stevens. "Yup, yup, I've seen it done, sure enough happen to me," said Ray.

"Funny thing though, I bet those young people haven't realized they are both in love yet," said Doc. With that the Doc up ended the bottle and took a big swig and then handed the bottle to Ray still lying on the examining table.

"I am really not a drinkin or cussin man," said Ray Stevens. "But then again, I am not writing this story, am I?"

"I'll just have to say and do whatever them cantankerous, tetchy, belligerent, no account writers make me say and do. I sees um both Randy and Bob there, pointin and laughin at me because of what and how I am sayin things and what it is I'm a doin. Well, boys, payback time will be comin. I'll tell the preacher and my wife to read this, and they will be setting two smarty pants fellas straight. Think on that, boys. They are my backup. She is the love of my life, my precious and loving wife. Hey, I made up a rhyme. Honey, oh Honey, I got something in this book I think you need to read," said Ray, smiling and nodding his head.

The crowd was disbursing, and in less than 10 minutes Sheriff Wilkins and his deputies were escorting Mr. Lip-shits, Mr. Slab-field, and Oliver Shag-nasty to the courthouse.

The Judge said, "You men caused a riot here in town. An innocent man might have been hung today. If it were not for one woman who believed this man to be innocent, we would have become a town of disgrace. I can fine you, give you a stiff jail sentence, or if I am of a mind to give you . . . ." The Judge stopped and hesitated. "I need to think on it for a while. Put these men in your jail, Sheriff. I will pass sentence in my own good time."

Sheriff Wilkins said, "They are really good men here in our community, Judge. I think they were just carried away with the moment."

The Judge then said, "Now that I think on it, you three will buy paint and brushes and paint the jail and the schoolhouse. You will do it for the fine and the time it takes you to complete the work." He hit the gavel down and said, "Court adjourned."

"You men are free to go. But come Monday morning, you need to be at work by

9 a.m. That jail needs painting. The schoolhouse—that building should be painted in no more than 3, well maybe 5 days at the most, no matter however long it takes. You will all be expected to formally apologize to the school teacher and Jon Dalton," said the Honorable Judge Leonard Monteleone.

Chapter Twenty-One

The judge had asked that the telegram be returned to Susan. She later gave the crumpled and now slightly torn telegram that was held in her hand as she had run up the main street to Jon to read for himself.

A lengthy telegraph message from Mr. William E. Wilson, President of the Fifth Bank of Denver and Vice President Mr. Pete Smyte, confirmed the names Jon and Frank Dalton, bank deposits, real estate papers in the carpetbag and how to remove them. Confirmation from the bank of the amount of money released to Jon and Frank Dalton. STOP

Susan told Jon she had taken it upon herself to send another telegraph to the Fifth Bank of Denver, Colorado, attention Mr. William E. Wilson. EMERGENCY Life or Death. Referring to herself as a Clerk of the Court. She did not see a quick reply, so she sent a second telegram, a duplicate of the first, except Attention: Bank Officer in Charge, intercepted by Vice President Peter Smythe. This was the response she received from the Denver telegraph office, sent by Mr. Pete Smythe. She had received and was carrying it when she saw the people pouring out of the Court House with every intention of hanging Jon for crimes she knew he didn't do.

Mr. Wilson had suffered a bad injury while fishing in the Colorado Rockies and was detained and had yet to return to work from his vacation.

"Three cheers for Mr. Pete Smythe, I know him personally. He ordered the security carpetbag." Jon said, "Susan, you went above and beyond to make this all happen and without you it might well have not happened. I owe you my life. I don't know how to repay you for doing what you did."

Jon actually had forgotten and neglected to tell Susan about the bank papers, the deposit records, and the withdrawal forms that were in the carpetbag, up inside the hidden false sides. Frank had originally packed the bag and was far more aware of the design and this specific area of the carpetbag. "I know, I surely, told the Sheriff about the hidden pocket in the carpetbag. He just didn't believe me."

"That was pure genius for you to send a telegram with the insistence from Susan B. Frost and refer to yourself as a Clerk of the Court. That was falsification and impersonating a Court official. That was a criminal act and could have gotten you in a heap of trouble if things had turned out differently. Shooting that man and discharging a firearm in the city limits causing bodily harm—that was a little extreme. You ever fire a pistol before?" asked Jon.

"My father taught me how to use a pistol and a rifle," said Susan. "I was excused of all charges by the Judge." Still dabbing at her nose with a handkerchief someone had given her, Susan said, "I am a mess. I need to excuse myself and go home."

"Yes, yes, of course. I need to go to the Sheriff's office and to the hotel and clean up as well. But, please allow me to buy your supper this evening at Del Veckeo's Italian Restaurant at 6 p.m.," said Jon.

"You have a date, but it's Del Monacoe's," Susan said. She realized she was starting to blush, so she turned and said, "I really must go, see you at 6."

Chapter Twenty-Two

J on was asked by the local preacher to come to their church to pray for Frank to be delivered from the coma. The Pastor asked Jon to have a short testimony ready to share when he was called forward.

The Pastor gave a brief explanation of Jon's most recent dilemma and the remarkable way God had delivered him from the very brink of death and the possibility of losing his life by hanging. The pastor talked briefly how Jesus was falsely accused and died in our place for the sins of all mankind. "Jon Dalton was also falsely accused, and we all surely know his story. It's the talk of the town. I am truly thankful for the outcome; and I say 'thank you,' church, for your prayers for Jon and his cousin Frank Dalton. I decided today to have Jon Dalton share with us his most recent trial, and together we can all pray for the healing of his cousin—that God will heal and deliver him from the coma that seems to have him bound. Mr. Jon Dalton."

"Ladies and gentleman, my name is Jon Dalton, and I am one very thankful child of God. I have been asked by your Pastor to give a short testimony. My cousin Frank is in need of our prayers. We all need to pray for him and ask God to deliver him from a thing Doc calls a coma. We will pray, but first I want to share some things with you."

"These verses are from the King James Version of the Bible. Read these verses along with me as I read them aloud."

John 3:16-17, "For God so loved the world that he gave his only begotten Son that whosoever believeth in him shall not perish, but have everlasting life. For God sent not his Son into the world to condemn the world: but the world through Him might be saved."

Romans 3:10, "As it is written, there is none righteous, no, not one."

Romans 3:23, "For all have sinned and come short of the glory of God."

Romans 5:8, "For God commendeth his love toward us, in that, while we were yet sinners, Christ died for us."

Romans 6:23, "For the wages of sin is death, but the gift of God is eternal life through Jesus Christ, our Lord.

Romans 10:9, "That if thou shalt confess with thy mouth the Lord Jesus and believe in thy heart that God raised him from the dead, thou shalt be saved." *(With the mouth.)*

Romans 10:10, "For with the heart man believeth unto righteous, and with the mouth confession is made unto salvation." *(With the mouth confession is made unto salvation.)*

Romans 10:13, "For whosoever shall call upon the name of the Lord shall be saved."

"If you believe, pray this prayer aloud. "Lord Jesus, I believe you died on a cross for all my sins, in 3 days you rose from the grave. I ask you to forgive me of the sins I have committed in my life. I here and now receive Jesus as my Lord and Savior. Fill me with the Holy Spirit of God to know your will. In Jesus name, Amen."

"I have a question for anyone who has received Jesus as your Lord and Savior who has strayed from God's path for your life. If you have any doubt or believe you need to know for sure, I suggest, you pray again aloud now, today. First read, I John 5:13, "These things have I written unto you that believe on the name of the Son of God; that you may know *(Know)* that you have eternal life, and that you may believe on the name of the Son of God."

Jon said, "How many of you understand these scriptures and want to pray aloud and become a child of God and make heaven your future home?" Many hands went up, so he said, "Let's all stand and every one of us will pray a prayer of salvation. Repeat after me, Father God in Jesus name, I ask you to forgive me of all my sins. I here and now ask Jesus to come in my life and be my Lord and Savior. I declare Jesus is Lord. I thank you, Father, that I am now saved as the Bible teaches. I also ask that my name be written in the Book of Life. In Jesus name, Amen."

"You need to come forward and stand here in front of the church. If you didn't know, but after the prayer tonight, you now believe, come forward and say a word. Many came forward, 11, including Susan the school teacher. Everyone said something about what he or she understood and why he or she had prayed. All listened and the congregation all applauded and cheered. All of the members of the church came forward and shook hands with and hugged those who prayed.

Now, standing in front of the small congregation, Jon said, "The next step is water baptism." He looked toward the Pastor and asked, "Pastor, how do you present baptism here at the First Baptist Church?"

The Pastor stepped to the pulpit and said, "The deacons will get the names of those who made a confession of faith tonight. Sunday morning after the message, we will conduct a baptismal service. For those of you who made a confession of faith here tonight, bring a change of clothes to be baptized."

"Jon, would you come to the platform. Jon and I with the deacons will all kneel on the platform and pray for Frank. I would ask every member to kneel in your pew right where you are and pray for him to be healed and delivered from the coma. I will pray aloud, and you all pray as you feel led of the Lord. This final prayer will conclude the service."

Chapter Twenty-Three

Two days later, early on Friday morning, Frank regained consciousness. He said he heard many voices saying his name and saying things that made him feel different, cared for and loved, unlike any time in his life. He was still weak, but he insisted on going to the Sunday morning service. He too went forward and prayed at the end of the service for rededication of his life to the Lord Jesus Christ. Frank was baptized along with the 11 that afternoon who had received Jesus as Lord at the end of the Wednesday evening message.

He mentioned something that was a surprise to most of the congregation. "If this church can agree together and pray for one man in a coma, what other remarkable things can happen if this church prays like that this next Sunday in both worship services. You prayed for me just last Wednesday in the evening prayer service. I was healed by Friday morning. I thank you for your prayers, and I praise the Lord. How much can the power of God do through a church with that kind of powerful prayer agreement?"

Frank said, "You people surely know I really believe with all my heart, I am here today because of your prayers for me. I thank God for every one of you. I want to stand at the back door and personally thank every person who prayed for me. We need to share and be thankful for every day we are alive and well. I thank the Father God and Jesus that Jon was able to have you pray for him. We will forever be grateful for the Pastor and you people of God in this wonderful church. God bless you, each and every one."

With that, Frank went to the back doors of the church and took time to shake the hand and personally thank everyone. Frank probably hugged every man, woman, and child in that church at least once if not twice. It was a great time, and you could not have attended and not have been moved by the presence of God in the church.

Jon and Frank attended every Sunday morning and evening service and Wednesday evening prayer meeting until the day they left the city. It was never the same in that church, they were told. A revival meeting broke out in the church and lasted 2 full months.

Sheriff Al Wilkins was so moved by the people in the community, he was one of the most involved at the church.

Jon told Frank what Susan had done with the telegram and her forthright presentation to the local church. She was almost totally responsible for their freedom. We decided to pay her way to the college of her choice. We exchanged addresses, and promised to return or come back as she pleaded for Jon to do. "I will visit you this summer in southern Missouri in your home town of Lamar, Missouri," said Susan. "Jon, I really want to see you again. You don't need to pay any money for tuition to a school for me." Jon and Frank insisted it was the least they could do.

Chapter Twenty-Four

"We both wanted to repay you in some way. Your college tuition would be a very good investment. But that will be your decision—whatever you decide how to spend the money, we will leave that up to you. NO, NO, we have made up our minds. It's all been decided. I already planned to give you the money," Frank said. He had it already inside a leather bound folder just large enough to hold the bills, with two strips of leather to secure the leather envelope.

"I need time to think and check with colleges and universities. This is too big of a decision to make in just one afternoon. I have been given a teacher's dream. I will see you guys this summer if not sooner," said Susan.

She stepped forward and hugged Jon. Then she loosened from her hug, and as she moved her head back she hesitated. Looking straight at Jon, she simply kissed him full on the mouth. She then kissed Frank on the cheek. "Thank you both, and see you soon." Susan turned and walked away.

"She saved our bacon," said Frank, looking directly at Jon, with that smile that said more than words could tell. "I think that girl has strong feelings for you. She kissed you right on the mouth. I mean, she flat held her lips there for almost a minute."

"Shut up, Frank. It wasn't for a full minute, well, maybe 45 seconds," said Jon.

"Well, she is special, and she did you a favor when no one else believed you. She did what very few would have. You could have been hung for a crime you didn't commit. She is one of the prettiest women I have ever seen, don't you think? asked Frank. "I would be marrying that girl if I were you. Maybe not today, but soon," said Frank, smiling.

"How much did you give her?" asked Jon. "Five hundred dollars, that is quite a lot."

"From each of us $500, a total of $1,000," said Frank.

"Not really, that much?" said Jon.

"What's your life worth, your freedom, spending years in jail for a crime you didn't commit?" asked Frank. "Your name being Dalton, walking up to a bank at the very worst time?"

Jon said, "You can't really put a price on your freedom for the rest of your life."

"Let's not feel stingy hearted about giving money to Susan. She is one of a kind. She was willing to protect you to have your freedom. She shot that man, and she could have possibly died herself for defending your right to have evidence presented that eventually proved your innocence. Few men have had a hangman noose around their neck with a angry mob trying to hang them and walked away a free man as you did, Old Hoss. You know it wasn't luck, chance, or coincidence with that coming to pass as it did. It was the protective hand of God," said Frank.

Jon then said, "Jesus did more for us both, Frank, than we really know. I haven't had a chance to tell you all the details. A lot happened while you were unconscious, I was amazed with all that happened after I prayed and got right with the Lord. Frank, God, answered my prayers, and the prayers of the church."

"Well, he answered my prayers," Frank said, smiling from ear to ear.

"O yeah?" said Jon. "Why don't you tell me about that."

Frank said, "You're a child of the Lord God Almighty, Born Again, is that right, Jon? Well it looks like Jesus has answered my prayers as well. I have been praying for you, Jon boy, most all your life, and God has truly blessed us both. I have been praying for you for a long time, my boy, son of the Lord God Almighty, servant of the Lord Jesus Christ, Amen, and Amen!" said Frank. He hugged Jon and then held him in a headlock, rubbing his knuckles on Jon's hair and kissed him on the top of his head. "I love you, my brother. We are children of God, and you, Old Hoss, are a man that prays to God." Frank hugged and pounded Jon's back with open hands of joy and affection. Both men were truly just thankful to be alive with all their troubles behind them. "Let's go home to Lamar, Missouri, and stay there for a good long while."

Chapter Twenty-Five

" Sheriff Al Wilkins had this idea about the two of us carrying the carpetbag with all the money from the bank when we eventually leave this town. The sheriff took the original carpetbag concealed compartments idea and had something made up special but I haven't seen anything yet. The money and the carpetbag are still in the safe at the bank," said Jon.

"The Sheriff and I met with Judge Leonard Monteleone and the bank president Ned Bentley with the bank's attorney Mr. La-mar Gene Sphincter in his office. I was given two envelopes, one with the original bank papers from the Fifth Bank of Denver, Colorado. The second with trial documents clearing us both of all charges. You weren't tried in court, but your name did appear on the original arrest and court documents."

Jon continued, "I was found innocent of all charges, and you were declared innocent and found not guilty of any fault due to all evidence submitted. A letter from the Judge restating the Court's apologies for the inconvenience we faced and the fact we were Dalton's but were not in any way involved in the bank robbery. The charges were dropped and were entered as a part of the official court record; Frank and Jon Dalton were not any part of the Dalton Gang, also referred to as the Wild Bunch Gang."

The carpetbag was returned to the bank after the issues were settled on the street the last day of the trial. The entire contents were removed and counted. Jon and Frank verified the accurate count of all the funds, and they were still in the bag, They signed a statement prepared by the Bank Attorney Mr. La-mar Gene Sphincter, with the Bank President, Sheriff Wilkins, and Judge Monteleone witnessing the release of the evidence and notarizing all the documents. Sheriff Wilkins was concerned about future use of the now infamous carpetbag. He had an idea that might solve the problem, and he would gladly have the city donate the money to make the replacement items for the carpetbag.

"My question to you, Jon, is, do you really know or have any idea about what Sheriff Wilkins had in mind as a replacement for the carpetbag?" asked Frank.

"Yesterday afternoon the Sheriff sent me to the Mercantile to pick up a package in my name in care of Al Wilkins. It was wrapped in plain brown paper. I was told to take the package directly to the Sheriff's office. When I asked, Sheriff Wilkins said, 'Does it really matter? All will soon be reveled,' he hesitated and a smile came across his face, 'revealed right now.'"

"The two handmade saddlebags were leather and had a simple design and looked like any others I had seen. It was revealed to me they were not like any other saddlebags. The custom made saddlebags were Sheriff Wilkins' personal design. They were made with special leather flaps in the inner sides of the bags that fold down and secure slightly overlapping at the bottom of the bags, with a third piece of leather that closed down on top of the two side panels, securing the side panels. The precision leatherwork was that of a real craftsman. The hidden area could secretly hold many straps of bills, with room in the center part of the saddlebags to place personal items. The designed secret compartments were all done to Al's specification. 'This gift for you and Frank is my way of saying I'm sorry for the trouble and grief I put the two of you through. Actually, just you, Jon. Frank was indisposed during the entire incident,' said Al."

"You were just doing your job, and a mighty fine job you were doing, I might add," said Jon.

"Yeah, well, I might have found out too late from a telegram from a Colorado Banker. I had a man tried for a crime, and found guilty by a jury. The sentence being swiftly carried out by vigilante justice, the city would have had a hanging in the street in front of the court house. To find out the truth just moments before, or a short time later that we had hung an innocent man. To later inform his next of kin, as it were who may or may not have recovered from a coma. 'We hung Jon Dalton, your relative, who we have since found out to have been an innocent man. We will just be biding you good day. You're free to go. Here's your hat. Have a good day.' I just thank God for how it did turn out," said Al Wilkins.

"I could have searched a little more diligently in the carpetbag and found a bank withdrawal form in the name of Frank and Jon Dalton, Fifth National Bank of Denver. This all wouldn't have happened. I allowed a young man who was zealous, but did not have the maturity to apply level headed judgment. I should have spent more time investigating myself. I had an underlying feeling things were not as they appeared. I should have listened to my heart," said Al. "We are all innocent until proven guilty. The system proved you guilty and you were innocent, Jon," he said.

"The first Continental Congress was attended by delegates from all but one of the first colonies. Men like George Washington, who was the official moderator and who was barred from voting due to his position, Thomas Jefferson, John Adams, and Benjamin Franklin were godly men who established the need for and created the Declaration of Independence, signed July 4, 1776. This body of men added the Constitution, ratified into law September 7, 1787. The first Ten Amendments became the Bill of Rights."

"I wonder what they would have thought if they had been visiting our town, our court house, that day and observed the incident that transpired out in the street after the trial. I wonder if those men were somehow able to periodically visit the House of Representatives or the U.S. Senate in Washington, D.C., to observe what has happened and what will happen in years to come as this country strives to govern itself like none other in this world."

"Benjamin Franklin answered a question asked by a local man that afternoon after he and others had signed the Constitution. 'Sir, I would ask, what have you men of the congress done for this country?'"

"Benjamin Franklin, walking from Carpenter's Hall in Philadelphia, Pennsylvania, said, 'We have given the people of these United States a Republic.' How many U.S. citizens have actually read the Constitution of the United States or the first Ten Amendments, called the Bill of Rights? How many American citizens have read the Bible? The very laws of this land are based on scripture," said Al. "'We have given the people of these United States a Republic.' How many people understand what it means to be a Republic? Republic means state, nation, democracy and freedom to rule, govern ourselves by laws, for the people, by the people, and of the people."

"The laws of this country—state, national, civil, or criminal laws, have a singularity of purpose and need proper law enforcement upheld by men who fill the positions of Deputy, Sheriff, Marshall, on a national level U.S. Marshall, elected and court-appointed Judges—men to do the job in an exemplary manner. We all have inalienable rights. We need not become moved by emotion, feeling, popularity of the crowd, and the circumstances to NEVER forget everyone is considered innocent until proven guilty," said Al Wilkins.

"Jon, do you know the definition of inalienable rights? I'll tell you. It means, unchallengeable, indisputable, not able to be forfeited rights that most people know not of."

Both men sat in total silence, and then Jon broke the silence as he said, "Sheriff, you did what you thought was right. You really could not have changed many or any of the events that happened in the last few weeks. You gave me your personal Bible, I read it, I prayed from it like I have never done before in my life. I have a spiritual closeness with the Father God, my Lord Jesus, and the Holy Ghost. I confess to my shame, I hadn't ever had such a closeness prior in my life. You had, what must have taken years of writing, handwritten notes throughout your Bible. They were a blessing to me. They encouraged me. What if this situation was God's way of getting me ready for something I need to do for myself or for someone else in the future? God's ways are past our finding out. If we can't trust God, who can we trust? We very seldom find ourselves in a situation where all we have is God. A man named Eli Harju, who I met in Missouri, said that phrase many times over: 'All we have is God.'"

"When I sat on that horse with a rope around my neck, I thought, 'Well, I am going home to heaven. You know I was sure of one thing, I'm saved, born again, a child of God, and heaven is my home. I am ready if I die.' I didn't want to die, but I was ready and I knew I was ready. Was I scared? You can bet your boots I was scared," said Jon.

"Well, giving you that Bible was probably the only right thing I did," said Al.

"Don't sell yourself short. The men who planned the hanging had everything planned out in advance. They knew they would have to get the drop on you and your Deputies and lock you in the jail as they did. If they hadn't, you and your Deputies, even Joe Caraway, would have stood between the violent crowd and the convicted man. No one in this city but God and Susan Frost, well maybe the telegraph agent, knew I was an innocent man, until Susan had it revealed to everyone in front of the court house as she did," said Jon.

"Why would you and your Deputies stand between me and the crowd that wanted a hang me? Because even a convicted man still has rights and due process of the law. A future date would have been set for sentencing for punishment to fit the crime. I would be sentenced to time in prison. A sentence of death is usually reserved for killing someone. The court trial found me guilty of bank robbery. If I had been guilty, I would have had to spend time in some place like Yuma Prison for a period of years."

"Al Wilkins, you are a good and honest man, a remarkable Sheriff. If you weren't, you wouldn't be beating yourself up for the few things you might have done differently. I thank God for men like you. Hopefully, you and I will be friends for the rest of our lives. I want to be life-long friends," said Jon.

"Thank you, Jon. You are a Christian gentleman, and I respect you for the living witness you exhibited throughout this situation," said Al Wilkins.

"Susan Frost, did you hear what she did?" said Jon

"I have been told and retold by more than one person. It's become the talk of the town," said Al.

"Thank you for the remarkable saddlebags for Frank and me. They are beautiful," said Jon.

"You are welcome," replied Al. "I just want to ask you again to forgive me for the presumptuous behavior I exhibited concerning your arrest and all I allowed you to go through."

Jon raised his hand to stop his comments. "First, no apology necessary. Mr. Al Wilkins, you are a good and honest man. You were just doing your job. Enough said."

A nod of his head, "Exactly, enough said," said Al.

The Sheriff and Jon took all the money from the carpetbag and placed it in the two saddlebags. It fit with a little to spare. They then placed the empty box that had held the two saddlebags into the carpetbag.

Jon took a strap of bills and handed them to Al.

"What is this for," Al asked.

"It's for you to invest in your life, start a business—a leather shop that sells saddlebags like the two you designed for Frank and me. A leather shop that sells saddles, bridals, chaps, vests, hats, quirts, and buggy whips with the name of ranch or owner of the horse embossed on the saddle or the cowboy's name carved on his chaps. Take the money. You could go to college and study law and become an attorney. You want to work as a Sheriff all your life? As you grow older and make no more or no less a month to live on—just enough to get by. Some night you make your rounds, and some crazy shoots you in the back. The Dalton Gang—the Dalton men were lawmen before they turned to a life of crime," said Jon.

"A short time ago I was sitting on a horse with a rope around my neck. I had this carpetbag with lots of money in one of the bank safes here in your fine city. A lot of good it would have done me or anyone else if I were hanged by my neck until I was dead. Take the money; take some time to travel to think what you would like to do. Travel to St. Louis, Chicago, Washington, D.C., or go to Philadelphia and see where the Declaration of Independence was signed. Do you want to go to school to pursue a specific career? Do you want to find a wife, buy a home, and raise a family? Perhaps you will meet a beautiful young lady, get married, and have three children and grandchildren."

"I might need a receipt or a letter for the reason I have come into so much money," said Al.

"Give me a blank piece of paper, pen, and ink. I will write out a statement for you. 'A financial gift from Jon and Frank Dalton for a business partnership, a possible venture of a leather shop or the business opportunity of your choice. These funds need not be accounted for, paid back, or returned.' I just signed and dated this letter. I suggest you get a deposit slip, go to the bank and make a deposit. Better yet, stick it in your shirt or stick it in the inside pocket of that fine jacket over there."

"I could go to a seminary and become a preacher," said Al.

"You have been a banker and a Sheriff. If you are called of God to be a Preacher, you should be a Preacher," said Jon. Both laughed, "Enough said?"

They carefully slipped the saddlebags back in the brown paper wrapper, minus the shipping label. Jon took the package to his room at the hotel. He packed folded clothes and some food supplies to eat on the way home into the carpetbag. Both saddlebags were ready to be placed one on each of the horses.

"Frank, the Doc just released you to ride horseback due to your need of complete healing. The horses we rode into this city a little over 2 months ago are over in the Livery Stable. I have paid everything in full at the hotel and the Livery Stable. I paid some extra for the good care of the horses. For the last month or so the horses have been grazing in a pasture behind the home of the Livery Stable owner. They were also taken out and ridden some by the Livery owner and his older sons." Jon said, "The horses were getting a little frisky out in the pasture with no one riding them. You know what they say, 'If you want to dance, you have to pay the fiddler.'"

"What does that mean?" asked Frank.

"The horses are all ship-shape and ready to go," said Jon.

"I take a few weeks off, go into a coma, and you get all philosophical on me," said Frank.

"What's philosophical mean?" said Jon.

"I don't know—it's a school teacher word," said Frank.

Early the next morning about an hour after sunrise, Jon and Frank rode their horses down the road to the east. The Dalton trial was old news and was now overshadowed by the day-to-day bustle of the little town in southern Kansas. The sun was warm and the removal of Jon's coat made it a little more comfortable as he rode to the right of Frank.

A lone horse and rider were hard to determine at first. The horse was standing just out from the trees on the right up the road about 200 yards. It appeared someone was waiting on horseback by the right side of the road. The rider was not a large man, and it appeared he had a large carpetbag hung on the side of the saddle and a larger than normal bed roll tied behind his saddle. The rider moved forward as the two men come closer.

Chapter Twenty-Six

It was not a man at all. It was Susan. She was dressed in riding clothes, and looked as if the outfit was just purchased from the local haberdashery. "Hello, guys. Care if I ride along with you today? It's not safe for a woman to be unaccompanied as she travels." She guided her horse between the two men. "I am off to check out some schools in the Kansas City, Missouri, area. I have an aunt and uncle in Independence. I stayed with their family when I was completing my studies in Grandview, Missouri. I will write a letter and see if I can rent a room and stay with them while I attend a school in the Kansas City area."

"I am originally from Kansas City, Missouri. Jon, have you thought about college? There's a good Law School in Independence," said Susan.

"I was thinking of studying Criminal Law and Business Law," said Jon. "If I am ever in a court room again, I want to know everything a man can know about the law. The innocent man deserves a lawyer who can defend him with knowledge and insight to bring all the facts to the case and have him proven innocent if he is innocent and investigate who the real criminal is in the situation."

"I couldn't agree with you more, Mr. Jon Dalton," said Susan smiling.

"As beautiful as any woman could smile," thought Jon.

"You might need an investigative legal assistant to help you in your law practice," said Susan.

"Frank, how are you feeling today? You still feel a little weak from the time you spent in the coma, laying on your back at the Doctor's office? You remember anything, or was it all just darkness?" asked Susan.

"We need to get to know each other with the possibility of me being kin folk and all. I hear tell your cousin Jon is getting married. You would be the best man, I would imagine—Jon's first choice for his best man."

"What about this, Jon? Something happen while I was out?" asked Frank.

"We might as well fill you in because we both have a big part to play in what happened. We are the major players in this story so we both need to tell you. No, I mean about getting married and all Susan is talking about. Frank, the truth is," said Jon, "yes, I am in love with Susan Frost, the school teacher—the woman we both owe our lives to. She was the force behind getting me set free from the false charges that you and I were facing. If it were not for her, you and I wouldn't be riding out of town today. I would have swung from a rope and be dead. Oh, I'd be in heaven, but dead just the same."

Jon said, "Wait a minute, everyone off their horses. Frank, I need you to hold the horses; and I need to do something." Jon helped Susan down from her horse. Taking her hand, he led her a few steps away from the horses. He knelt down on one knee and said "Susan Mary Frost, I, Jon Dalton, am asking for your hand in marriage. If I need to ask your father for your hand in marriage, I will gladly do so. Susan Mary Frost, will you marry me?"

Susan said, "Yes, Jon Dalton, I will marry you."

Moments later, the three were again all on horseback. "You will need to meet the family," said Jon. All three rode slowly south and east in the direction of Lamar, Missouri, home of Jon and Frank Dalton. They both had stories to tell that would make relatives laugh and cry. Susan, Jon's fiancée, would be introduced to the family and a wedding planned. Then the young couple could have a honeymoon wherever they wanted. Next, it was off to Kansas City for some higher learning.

Jon did become an attorney. Susan graduated with a double major in English and Education from a university. She was a degreed professional. She audited many legal and law courses and became an excellent paralegal secretary and court recorder. Jon practiced law the majority of his life in Kansas and Missouri, with the assistance of Susan his wife, the most adept paralegal secretary.

They lived out their days in a way that they could have only dreamed of at any time before in their young lives.

This is truly not the END.

A new life and a bright future had just begun for Susan Frost Dalton, Jon Dalton, and of course Frank who was not just going along for the ride. The three of them were young and full of ambition, and all three had a dream that would most assuredly come to a sure reality. Frank liked to refer to their assets by saying, "We are just well to do, always down play your worth, never draw attention to things that make others curious." Jon would say, "Some people who live near us are very wealthy." Maybe, just maybe, Susan had a sister." Frank could only hope.

The End? Well, perhaps a continuation to the next part of what appears to be a never-ending story.

This appears to be the beginning for Mrs. Susan Frost Dalton and her husband Mr. Jon Dalton. They are truly both lucky sorts.

A Final Summation for Part 1 of the series of three Parts

Frank and Jon returned to Denver and the cities of the Front Range many times in their lives. This story I was told in 1920.

Jon Dalton with his grandson and his wife drove the car they were given by Jon as a wedding present. They borrowed a small trailer and a burrow from a man Jon knew in Denver. With a trailer hitch attached to the trailer and the purchase of food and supplies, the three Daltons and the burrow were off. They had maps that Jon had made from prior trips into this remote area showing a few logging roads which were just narrow one lane trails cut into the forest by woodsmen who were harvesting trees on a hillside a good day's walk from the entrance to Lost Park. It was in this area the car and the trailer were left under a tarp with a note attached.

The threesome then packed the burrow with the food and provisions needed for a 3-week stay in the area of the mine. The three each wore a backpack as instructed by Jon. It still took 2 days to walk to the mine. With the composition and the detail in the original letters of Frank and Jon Dalton, the location of the mine was easily found. The exact location was found from a detailed drawing completed years before by Jon. The simple process of reading an engineer's hand compass from the highest point of three peaks was triangulated and were lined up with three lines crossing within 50 feet of the location of the mine.

Jon could have walked to the exact location, but he was thrilled to be a part of the excitement and enthusiasm of the young couple as they found the mine for the first time for themselves. The stone marker at the base of the entrance was still readable with the chiseled first initials "F & J Dalton" and date "May 1, 1891." Apart from the concrete marker that Jon swept clean with a small Swiss broom, the hillside looked to be part of the brush-covered overgrown mountainside. Jon used a small tree branch to dig in the dirt and remove the hard packed soil and the small rocks that were slowly cleared away. Even then the area looked like the side of the mountain.

Jon slowly placed his fingers in the base of the rocks. A small door was pulled and then slid open, and the wood frame of ax-hewn logs that fit perfectly made with meticulous precision was exposed. The concrete on the top and the sides was reinforced with iron pieces to give strength and lasting durability. The opening was just large enough for a man to enter on his hands and knees crawling as it were. Inside near the entrance of the mine was a nail and hanging from it was a small leather bag with a small notebook inside where recorded names and dates of times the mine had been entered and the amount of dust removed. Only Jon and Frank had made entries and were listed.

Camp was set up. The small gray burrow was staked out to graze with a long rope to keep him from running off. The 20 days brought a production of about 90 pounds of high-grade gold dust and small pieces of the type of ore the mine yielded. The ore was heated and melted into small button shapes and placed in the bags Jon had in his backpack.

The three left with about 30 pounds each securely placed on the back of the burrow. Jon made sure all understood there were three equal shares for the combined effort. The price that gold was sold and purchased for in 1925 for premium gold in ounces was $21 a troy ounce. This was a joint effort and each one of the three would benefit a yield of 30 pounds each, worth about $16,000 plus or minus. It was Jon's intention to give this young couple each 30 pounds for a combined amount of 60 pounds. This would help them pay for life's expenses, to gain a highly paid position because of a college education, buy a house, invest in property, raise a family, and most of all, live well. The total sum of the two equal shares of the raw ore was $32,000 and would do just that.

The only thing Jon asked was to keep the mine a secret. The original promise was to tell just one person. Frank had told one person, and that was his cousin Jon. Jon had not told anyone all these years, so he decided he would tell his grandson and he would or should tell his wife. The couple did return twice after the initial time, and a third time to reveal this location to one person. Who was this person? A relative of the woman who married Jon's grandson. It was yours truly—it was me; I have yet to tell anyone. I am thinking I need to do just that. It's 2011, and what is the price of gold by the troy ounce today July 25, 2011?—*but lest we forget, this is a work of fiction. Is there really a place I have mentioned, or is it all in my imagination?*

Part 2

The Daltons: Lawmen In-Laws
and Outlaws

Character profiles with background and general information

Laurence "Larry" Crow Dalton, Sr., was a Town Marshall, and later became a County Sheriff in one of Illinois' 200 counties. Larry was intelligent with a depth of reasoning ability and a photographic memory. The Dalton men were tall in stature— 6' 1" to 6' 3" and 205 to 230 pounds. Their facial appearance had sharp, lean features and high cheekbones. The Dalton men had a personality which was fair, honest, strong-willed, and domineering with a purpose-driven nature.

Larry, Sr., and his father inter-married with local indigenous women. The Indian people who lived in the area were believed to be direct descendants with ancestral linage to the Cahokia people of southern Illinois who were called the Mound Builders.

Larry, Sr's., grandfather was a surveyor and the son of one of the original landowners in the territory. Larry's father expanded their total land holdings upwards to and beyond 4,004 acres. This land was a combination of wooded forest, rolling hills, open grassland, ponds, and streams. Larry, Sr., married Lorena, a Cahokia. They were cousins through marriage, not blood relatives. They met, fell in love, and were married for some 54 years until her death.

Laurence "Larry" Smith Dalton, Jr., born February 26, 1855, was the third born son of Town Marshall Laurence Crow Dalton, Sr., and mother Lorena Faye Smith Dalton. Lorena had a Scot/Irish father, and her mother was a full-blooded Cahokia Indian. Lorena's mother called herself Crow Woman. Crow Woman was affectionately referred to as "C" by her husband, family, and friends.

Richard "Rich" Smith Dalton was the identical twin brother of Laurence, of slender build and agile. Rich was born 12 minutes after Laurence, making him the younger brother. Rich spent many of his growing up years with the Cahokia people of his mother.

Laurence and Richard are one-fourth blood of the indigenous people and are considered half breed or half breeds.

Laurence "Larry" Smith Dalton, Jr., is so named due to a custom to give the last name of his mother or her maiden name as a middle name to a son. This is also a way some whites name their sons and daughters.

Larry was 17 years old on his first trip west in the summer of 1872. Larry met and became friends with Dark Wind, a young brave of the Sioux tribe. Larry's second trip west was when he was a U.S. Marshall working with the Pinkerton's pursuing a train robber in the year 1891.

Cletus Jonas Magnus was a local blacksmith, owner and proprietor of the Magnus Livery, Hay, and Feed Store in the city of Kerwin, Kansas. He was called by the nickname "Skeeter" by all who knew him. Cletus had a wife named Mary Elizabeth "Lizzy" Shepherd Magnus. They had two children—a boy Timothy 'Tim' Shepherd Magnus (6 years old) and a baby girl Leatha Lovice Shepherd Magnus (18 months old).

Mary Elizabeth "Lizzy" Shepherd Mangus, Cletus's wife, played poker. Her father was a professional gambler for the last 30 years of his life. Theodore "Teddy' Shepherd taught his daughter how to play many games of chance, including many card games. She was very proficient. She practiced for years and knew all of her father's tricks. Lizzy had a female friend Josie Josephine Wilkins. The two women had a poker game they operated from time to time for fun and profit.

Josie Josephine Wilkins, the older of the two women, worked in the Café/Saloon as a bartender, manager-bouncer. She was a woman of good character and was respected by all who worked with her and knew her. She attended the Methodist Church every Sunday.

Josie promoted and officiated at the high stakes poker games Mary Elizabeth Mangus played. The games were usually played in a private room in the hotel two buildings down from the saloon. Her job at the game was to be the official overseer, bouncer, and ramrod for the poker games. She also dressed the part in blue jeans, boots, flannel shirt, hat, and a side arm. For the final touch as a disguise, she sometimes wore a full mustache. The true identity of this burley bouncer was never linked to any who ever knew this unidentified local.

Josie had worked in a carnival for many years. She became proficient in the way of life few could comprehend or ever master. The long list includes such things as sharp shooter and promoter of semi-professional boxing events. The first summer at the age of 12 she was a clown. The art of facial makeup paid life-long dividends. Her full name is Henrietta Josephine Wilkins. She didn't like her first name, took the name of her father Joe, and called herself Josie.

She eventually shared her large home with Cletus, Mary Elizabeth, and family—one of the most expensive homes in the town. The three eventually promoted numerous endeavors that were famous for drawing large crowds and were undoubtedly profitable in all parts of the Colorado, Nebraska, and Kansas territories. It was never disclosed how much money was actually made by the two ladies from the immense proceeds made from the years of conducting the high stakes poker games. Josie was a lady of many talents, healthy, and alert into her senior years until her death in her late 90's.

Peter Huffington was owner and proprietor of the trading post at the North Platte, Nebraska, Union-Pacific Railway Office; and sole owner of the K Bar B-Q Ranch north and east of North Platte, Nebraska, believed to be in the thousands of acres of open range.

Del Waldrip was Sheriff of Hill Dale, Kansas. He was cold, calculating, very professional, and 5' 9" 180 pounds. He was Sheriff of other frontier towns including Dodge City, Kansas, and Fort Hays, Kansas. Del was starting his fifteenth year as a town sheriff.

Billy Wilson was the Sheriff of Salina, Kansas, except for the 4 years he worked with and assisted a close friend as the Deputy Sheriff of Kerwin, Kansas. Billy Wilson was 6' 2" tall, slender, black hair, pointed features with a weak chin, thin frame, and muscular body. His keen wit and lightening fast draw put many a man behind bars or dead in the local boot hill cemetery. He had a wife named Sharon. She was exceptionally beautiful, striking in her appearance with shoulder length red auburn hair, was highly intelligent, and an accomplished pianist.

Little Elk, sometimes called Black Wind, was a Native American youth of about 16 years in the year 1872, almost 5' 9". Laurence met Little Elk on the open range west of Hays, Kansas, in the Kansas-Colorado territory on his first trip west. Little Elk had been thrown from his horse and lay semi-conscious when Larry Dalton found him on the open prairie June 15, 1872. Larry took the young Indian and nursed him back to health, saving his life from a certain death on the open prairie from exposure and possibly starvation.

They remained together for the rest of their lives, separating for short times for one reason or another. The bond between the two men only grew stronger as the years passed. The two friends shared many adventures throughout their colorful lives—from the chance meeting on the Kansas-Colorado plains to the mountains of Colorado in Central City and Black Hawk. Their names first translated with the universal sign language both were using made the name "little" in Larry's mind. The word "little" actually means unassuming, reserved, and humble to the Sioux. Little Elk's height was not considered to be short of stature among his people.

Toby Kermier Rhireson was storekeeper and owner of the general store at Fort Hays, Kansas.

William "Willie" Townsend Myers was the blacksmith and owner of the livery stable in Fort Hays, Kansas. Larry Dalton traded his first lame horse to this Smithy on his first trip west. Willie sold two mules to Larry. A civil war letter spoke of two mules named Sprit and Tate.

Wanted Poster: Franklin "Frank" Beesley Rodgers of southern Missouri. Height 5' 8"; weight 165 to 175 pounds; hair brown, some gray; eyes blue; a narrow scar on the right cheek from the top of the ear to lower jaw. He wears a fedora, black suit and tie, two white ivory-handled revolvers, and tie down holsters. Served/worked with U.S. Army Corps of Engineers, worked as a Civil

Engineer, worked as a private contractor in Southern U. S. and Central America. A tenured College Professor of Drury College, Springfield, Missouri.

This man is wanted for questioning concerning a payroll train robbery on the Burlington Northern & Santa Fe Railroads June 15, 1877. Reward of $1,000.00 is offered for any information leading to the arrest and conviction of this man. He should be considered armed and dangerous. Contact Pinkerton's office, Grand Central Train Station, St. Louis, Missouri, Terminal Annex building, second floor. Special Agent Philbert L. Wesley.

Chapter One

The sun was just slipping out from under a large puffy cloud domed and billowing out from the north to the south. I could see the heat coming up from the ground, up to and over the western horizon. The mountains were stretching out to the north, disappearing as miniature dots on the horizon. The same range of mountains to the south, but different in shape and size, spread out before me until they diminished to mere specks on the northern horizon.

I was unable to ride my bay colored mare. I had walked the animal into Salina, Kansas. After inquiring the location of the only livery stable, I stood outside the Magnus Livery, Hay, and Feed Store and yelled "Hello!" I was standing there waiting, and before I could yell another "Hello," I found myself looking at a big man wearing faded blue denim overalls, scuffed dirty boots, and no shirt. I cleared my throat and said, "I have a horse here I am afraid might have gone lame. I dismounted and have been leading her for over an hour."

The owner, Cletus Jonas Magnus, better known as "Skeeter," took the reins and led the horse into the cool darkness of the large barn. A cat scurried from behind the wooden gate of an open stall and disappeared out the back door of the building.

I watched as the big man was kneeling down and pressing his fingers into the leg of the mare. He made partial word sounds as he examined the right and left fore legs. He then led the mare out into the corral and watched as she walked—showing signs of a slow hesitation in her step and again a response to a tenderness as the Smithy touched her leg.

Barn sparrows were heard but not seen, high up in the rafters chirping out a melodious conversation understood only by them. Perhaps an intruder to their lofty domain—a stray cat—was near listening to the chatter and using the sound to locate an unsuspecting sparrow and moving ever so slowly for the unseen attack to capture a mid morning snack. My mind was drawn back to the Smithy when I heard him say. "I spect this animal will possible never recover iffen you had rode her any more than you did." He then stood there staring with no real expression on his face, then ever so slowly a smile came across his round face. "So what ya want me to do fer ya?"

"I need a fresh mount. I am heading west, and I really don't know what I am going to do if I don't get me another animal." I looked down and kicked the toe of my boot in the dirt of the hard packed soil, and waited in silence.

The blacksmith took his arms and slid them inside the upper part and behind the suspenders of the overalls he was wearing. "I have a mule there in the corral I'll sell ya, fer, aah, $30. That horse of yorn might never be able to ride again. I'll keep um, probably have to put her down," he said, looking down shaking his head.

"I can't, I won't," I said. "I'll just take my horse down the street to that other livery stable." I bit off my words remembering the telling of there ain't but one livery here in this town. I quickly said, "I'll find a local rancher and trade this one for a good horse. Better yet, I'll tell the sheriff the predicament I am in and see what he thinks about what you just told me. My horse is worth three mules," I said, with my finger now pointing straight in the face of the blacksmith.

"Wait! Wait, boy! No need to get all in a snit. I now see you knows somethin bout horse flesh. I sell the mule for $20 and give you $10 to boot for your horse. What ya say? Your horse might recover from being lame iffin I care for her good and proper."

"She may? You mean, she will definitely recover, and you will sell her for $40 or $50 or more, no problem, right?" I said.

I followed the Smithy through the barn and out into the corral and removed the saddlebags, saddle, and the bedroll from the mare. "You get the mule and the $10, and I'll saddle up the mule, and we'll have a deal." I was just finishing tightening up the cinch on the mule when the blacksmith walked towards me with the $10 in his out—stretched hand. I took the money and placed it in the pocket of my shirt. I removed the bridal from the mare and slipped it on the head of the mule. I quickly realized I needed to extend the cheek strap on the bridal before I could place it on the mule. With the proper adjustment, I slipped it in place over her ears and behind her jaws. The bay mare made a noise, and I turned and placed my hand on the side of her head. She made another sound as she usually had in the evenings as we had spent time together moving west out on the open prairie.

"She is a pretty girl," said the blacksmith. He was now looking at the smooth lines, appearance, and shape of a remarkable mount now standing in front of him.

"Worth far more than 10 dollars and a mule," I said.

"Yeah, maybe, iffen she hadn't come up lame and all. Time, time will tell," he said slowly.

"Look at her teeth, and tell me what you think," I said, looking directly at the man.

He placed his hands on the sides of her head and took a quick look, and said, "Damn, she is a beauty and not that old."

"She is lame now, but I walked her as soon as I noticed she was making signs she might be going lame. She will soon be fine and make you far more than $10 and the price of this mule." I said, smiling and shaking my head.

I mounted the mule and said, "You open the gate, and I'll be on my way."

The blacksmith said, "I might just keep her and train her to pull a surrey. I just bought one. Gonna sell it to the Doctor. I parked it over there." He pointed to the buggy just outside the back of the corral."

"She would make a fine looking carriage horse for anybody, and especially for a Doctor." I touched the brim of my hat and nodded to the blacksmith.

The bay made that same familiar noise, and moved her head up and down three times. "She must have really liked you," said the blacksmith.

"Next you will tell me she is saying, 'Good Bye,'" I said. I slid off the mule and approached the bay. She pushed her head up under my arm and breathed out with what would appear to be a heavy sigh. "You will be ok, girl. This man is a good horse man, and he will teach you to be the Doctor's carriage horse. I walked with my mule through the gate the blacksmith was holding half open now. The bay came and placed her head over the now closed gate and made a loud whinny.

"I'll be," said the blacksmith, "she is smart."

"The perfect Doctor's carriage horse," I said.

"Well, she is lame; I was takin that in account when I offered you the $10 and the mule."

Sitting there staring down at the mule, I thought to myself, "The mule is a female, all mules are female. She is larger in her size and shape than some mules I have seen." I turned in the saddle and said to the Smithy, "I am sure in your heart you feel you made a good deal, right?"

"Yeah, she is a beauty. I knew she was all along. You are right, kid."

The mare had stumbled twice out on the open range. The second time I fell off, head over breakfast, landing on my back on the ground. I had great concern she might be stumble footed. A carriage horse with only a carriage to pull and no weight on her back even running full out, she might never stumble again. "Well, I wouldn't take that to the bank," I thought.

I turned back in the saddle and touched the mule in the flanks with the heels of my boots, and she stepped right out. Soon we moved west out of town.

My mind was momentarily distracted when I heard a woman's voice singing in a house off to my right. I listened to the singing as I continued to ride west. As the voice faded, I thought, "I haven't heard a woman singing just because she was happy with her life, singing by herself, in her house all alone. Horses and animals I understand. Women, on the other hand, who really understands a woman? I have seen some ladies, and I have seen some women. God made nothing prettier or fairer on His green earth and that's the truth." I might have me one sometime—a real full time nighttime girlie girl.

As I rode on, a thought came to me—I might need a name for this mule. Let's see, what would be appropriate? "Jennie the mule—no, no, that's not even original. Half the mules in Missouri are probably called Jennie," I said aloud.

I was about 300 yards from the west edge of the town when I heard the sound of horse's hoofs coming up from behind me. I turned in the saddle. I should have been surprised, but I wasn't. The bay mare stopped up short and gave a low whinny and a snort. She then stared, slowly moving her head up and down.

I threw a lasso around her neck and was riding back into the town when I saw the blacksmith stepping into the saddle of another horse to move out into the street. I shouted to him, "How'd she get loose to come running after me?"

"I opened the gate and she bolted right through and was down the street after you before I could stop her," he said.

I handed the blacksmith the rope, and he dismounted and walked the mare through the barn and out into the corral. He came back and took the saddle off the mount he was planning on riding after the mare and was carrying it back into the tack room. "I have an idea," I said. "Put her in one of those stalls and give her some grain, some oats, or maybe some apple slices. Keep her inside for a day or so"

"That's just what I will do," said the blacksmith.

I stepped off the mule and tied her to the rail in front of the livery stable. I stood there and waited until the blacksmith stepped out into the bright sunshine. "It's getting late in the day, and I'm better off bedding down here than out on the prairie. You ever take a break to coffee up during the day?" I asked.

"Well, occasionally, but usually I jus work til noon and go home for lunch, back to work, and then home for supper in the evening. I usually place a small sign [BACK "N" 20 MINUTES] on the door iffen I'm gonna leave. I have a wife, she's a good cook, and my son and a baby girl. I eat lunch at home with um most every day," said the Smithy.

"Well, we need to talk, so I'll buy you a cup of coffee and I'll bend your ear for a while, if that's all right with you?" I said.

"Sure, where, ya wanna go?" said the Smithy.

"You got a café in this town?"

"Yeah, sure enough. You follow me, and we can go through and behind the buildings across the street and make our way right into the back door. It's part of the saloon," the Smithy said as he pulled on a shirt over the suspenders of his overalls.

We were between the buildings almost to the next street when the Smithy said "Wait. Let's go put your mule in out of the sun, ok?"

"Good idea, you wait here. We need not both go, I can do it. She's my mule, a man is only as good as he treats his animals," I said. I took the mule inside, removed the saddle and bridal, and opened the back corral gate. She walked slowly into the corral. I quickly walked back out into the sun, and we were off.

In no time we were having coffee and a donut made fresh by the cook. The waitress who was also the cook was now looking at both of us smiling and nodding her head. The Smithy gave her the thumbs up sign and said, "They are delicious." She then turned and disappeared into the kitchen.

I said, "You need to keep the mare in the stall for some time. I don't plan bringing her back from clear across the country tomorrow or next week." I took another bite of the best donut I had eaten in a while and a sip of the black coffee.

"I think so, too. I suspect you may be right—that mare is one powerful smart hoss," the Smithy said with his mouth full of donut. He then took another swig of coffee and washed down the remains of his last bite, and quickly bit off another.

"Hey, slow down. I know they are good. You'll eat them donuts and wish you had more," I said smiling.

"Why you bein' so nice to me? I'm just a blacksmith in a small sparrow fart town out here on the prairie," he asked, looking at me with that original dead stare.

"It's just I try to be honest and do the right thing. My father is a Sheriff in the state of Illinois, and he raised me right, to do right if the stars fall from heaven. That mare we traded for stumbled, and she pitched me off this morning. Then she came up lame, and I feel I need to tell you, that's all. You can call off the deal, and I'll give back the mule and the $10," I said, with a half smile and a nod of my head.

"Why she throw ya?" asked the blacksmith, talking with his mouth full of donut.

"She was spooked by a rattler snake. We ain't got any snakes like rattlers in Illinois. We got all kinds of snakes there. What I mean is we ain't got any like those rattlers. I was probably more afraid than the mare when I fell off and hit the ground. I just lay there, the wind all knocked out of me trying to roll total clear of the snake. I was thrown clear, but I was startled. Then I just watched the snake slither away."

The Smithy just looked at me and slowly started to smile and then laugh. "You silly fool, most horses would shy away from a rattler. She probably saw it foren you ever seen it."

"That horse will make a real fine carriage horse, and she will be treated for bein lame. She'll be fine in a few days. I'll clean her up, and she'll be shining after I rub her down good. I'll then sell her to the good Doctor, and he will be pleased to have her pulling that carriage. I'll keep the horse and his buggy for when he be needin it for his country rounds. I need to git some black paint to make that carriage look as good as new. I will make plenty of profit on the horse and the buggy. The Doc is probably the most well-to-do man here bouts."

The blacksmith finished his donut and swallowed his last gulp of coffee. He waved his hand when the waitress started over to give him a refill. "Thanks, no," he said. "I might have a job for a young man who is honest and I can trust," he said rubbing his hands on the legs of his coveralls. "You think you could go and pick up a string of horses 3 or 4 days' ride to the north of here? You would take my money and buy a string of horses from a big English ranch called the K Bar B-Q Ranch. Would you be up to takin a job like that for me?" asked the Smithy.

I just sat looking at the blacksmith. I said, "Why not train some local man to run the livery stable and go yourself? You can train someone in a few days. That's the best and the safest way. You know where the ranch is located, and it's your money. You have family, your wife, here in town. She can check on the man you train to run the livery. What could that possibly do to hurt your business?"

"Let me think?" he said. "To be honest with you, my wife is a good cook and she's a good wife, and I trust her. But the last time I left town to buy some riding stock, she took up with one of the gals at the saloon, and she was playing poker—mostly with the cowboys who came through, cattle drivers, and some of the locals. She made more money in the 2 weeks I was gone than I made in the livery in 2 months. She said she didn't do it for the money, she was just havin some fun."

"Her father was a professional gambler all his life and taught her all his tricks, and she learned pretty well. The woman at the saloon would dress in man's pants, plaid shirt, boots, and a side arm and put her hair up under her hat. Her friend is Josie Wilkins—she is one tough cookie. Josie worked at the saloon, and she would act as her agent and tell the men about this private card game and how and when the game was played. Josie took a percentage of the pots won for her promotion and protection for a fair and honest game."

"I knew something was wrong when I got back. Couldn't put my finger on it, so I just waited and everything came out. She gave me the money and was surprised I knew what had happened. One of the neighbor ladies, the town gossip, told me every detail. She was watchin and kept a written account of everything that happened. She attends the Baptist Church, and she makes it her business to know almost everything that happens in this town. The neighbor lady read from a diary 14 days of details. I asked iffn I could keep the dairy for a spell and never let on to my wife I knew everything. I told Lizzy that I knowed what she did and how long she was doin it. I said just what I needed to say, and Lizzy confessed to everything and insisted I take the money and invest it in the family business."

I told the blacksmith, "I am truly sorry to hear that. That must put a strain on the marriage. What business plan do you have, just staying here in town forever? You need fresh riding stock. Just buying and selling whatever comes riding down the street, charging for feed and hay as you board horses . . ."

"Well, now you see my predicament. I am damned if I go and coming up short on real business if I stay in town."

Chapter Two

"There must be something a man could do. Let me think on it. It's getting too late in the day; I will need to stay here tonight. How about I sleep here in the livery up in the loft, and let you know about me getting a string of horses for you. I will give you my decision in the morning," I said smiling. We walked back to the livery the same way we came. Two men were riding up and asked that their horses be tended to—feed, water, grain, and rub down. They were going to stay the night and needed their horses in the morning. I took the horses into the livery and said "I'll take care of the horses; you collect the four bits apiece for the services."

I was just finishing when the Smithy walked up. He said. "I usually charge two bits a piece. You said four bits apiece, and they both paid it and left happy. I just made twice my regular fee. Here's four bits for you. It's all I can do for your help."

"No, no sir," I said. "I am working off my night's lodging. You keep all that money. I'll start cleaning up and feeding these animals. You let me handle things around here. In an hour it will be time for you to go home and have dinner anyway."

"I'll go home and tell my wife you will be joining us for dinner. I'll tell her you might be helping with the livestock buying."

"No, let me think on it; and I will give you my final decision in the morning," I said. "I'll eat dinner at the café where we had coffee."

The Smithy walked over to me and stuck out his hand to shake mine. I felt the four bits in my palm. "Supper is on me, and this should help toward breakfast as well."

"Thanks, Boss," I said.

"That's what I like to hear," he said.

"I don't even know your name," I said.

"Well, sorry, I ain't introduced myself sooner. My name is Cletus, Cletus Jonas Magnus, but my friends call me Skeeter."

I said, "Laurence or Larry Smith Dalton, Jr., if we are being all official about it. I am a U.S. Marshall working my way west in pursuit of a man wanted for questioning concerning a private matter."

"Skeeter, I am on official business, and I would ask you keep everything I tell you about me being a U.S. Marshall on the Q.T. and tell no one until I have completed my business. I was thrown from my horse while in pursuit. I believe my suspect to be long gone heading south to Mexico—as he and any other wanted varmint usually does when he's a running and has someone hot on his trail." Skeeter stood looking at the badge I was holding out for him to see. "I need you to be totally trustworthy and not tell a living soul. As a favor for your secrecy and help, I will have your horses personally delivered here to your livery stable from the K Bar B-Q Ranch. My father and I met the owner of the K Bar B-Q Ranch in St. Louis last March when he was buying livestock. We became friends. He was buying some of the best horseflesh I have ever seen," I said, as I placed the badge in the inside vest pocket of my jacket.

"If you are serious about buying a string of horses from the K Bar B-Q Ranch, I can act as your agent and set it up for you with no problem. You can set up a bank transfer from your local bank here in town to the Dodge City Bank, Dodge City, Kansas. That's the bank Peter Huffington used to purchase the livestock we helped him select at the stockyards in St. Louis, Missouri. Peter Huffington is the sole owner of the K Bar B-Q Ranch north and east of North Platte, Nebraska. His ranch includes thousands of acres of open range. He also owns and operates the Trading Post in North Platte, Nebraska. His property is next to the Union-Pacific Railway Station and Train Depot next to the switching yard."

"Skeeter, do you have a bank account at the local bank here in town? No? No matter, you will have an account. Then we will transfer money to the bank used by the K Bar B-Q Ranch after we receive the horses delivered to your livery stable. Skeeter, can I trust you for complete silence on these matters—me being just a saddle tramp heading west and nothing more?"

Skeeter looked at me with that dead stare and said, "What are you talking about? I have no idea about anything you have just said. You are a saddle tramp that came through here, traded a horse, and I sold you a mule. I say, sir, you look to be a stranger and nothing more. I couldn't remember your appearance and or the mare you traded or the mule I sold you," said Skeeter. He gave a slight nod of his head and a quick wink.

"Well, I'll be leaving now and see you bright and early in the morning. Sleep tight and don't let the bed bugs bite, Mr. aah, Mr., well, what was his name?" He said to himself as he walked away. "I don't rightly know." Then to my surprise he returned and said, "Delivery of some riding stock here, to my door?"

"Yep," I said. "If you can never mention you know my real identity and my purpose for being here."

Skeeter smiled and said, "Oh, I can't say, because I don't know anything, not now—not ever." He walked away talking to himself. "I order them horses, and they are delivered. I have the money sent through their bank all clean and legal. I will just sign the papers. Oh, yes, I can do that; yes indeed."

Chapter Three

The next morning before I walked to the café where I was eating breakfast, I wrote two letters. The first letter was addressed to the K Bar B-Q Ranch in the northern Kansas southern Nebraska territory about 20 head of halter-broke riding horses at the price of low dollar per head inquiring of the low bid price. The second letter was addressed to the Dodge City Bank, Dodge City, Kansas, and the First Bank and Trust at the Union-Pacific Trailhead in Dodge City, Kansas, concerning a "Letter of Credit" and deposit from a wire to the bank in North Platte, Nebraska. The matter was the purchase of livestock from Mr. Peter Huffington, K Bar B-Q Ranch. With reference to the future possible sale of 15 to 20 horses to a Mr. Cletus Jonas Magnus, owner and proprietor of the Magnus Livery, Hay, and Feed Store of Kerwin, Kansas.

I had opened a personal/business account at the First Bank, Union-Pacific Trailhead, Dodge City, Kansas. I could fund the purchase of the horses for Cletus, and he could pay me back from the cash funds his wife gave him from her poker winnings. I would do this as a financier for an additional charge of 10 percent of the total amount of the purchase price. I would need to complete a third letter and outline the business proposal contract for services with my fee of 10 percent and any cost I might have incurred with the transaction with Mr. Cletus Jonas Magnus, his wife Elizabeth (the money lady), and myself.

I was joined by Skeeter just as I was finishing my last sips of black coffee. I told Skeeter what I had just set up in writing. I described in simple terms that I proposed for him to allow me to act as his agent for a simple 10 percent of the purchase price. We were setting into motion the purchase and delivery of his 15 to 20 head of prime riding stock.

This method of business is used in the banks of Europe and the banks of the east coast and most definitely in New York State. My father, who is a sheriff in Springfield, Illinois, has a very good friend—a bank president in St. Louis, Missouri—who trained me in business.

Skeeter said, in a rather flat tone. "Why not just ride up to the ranch, meet the owner, and ask if he has horses to sell? Walk to the corral and look over the horses in the corral. I pick out the horses I want, I pay the man cash. I have him write out a Bill of Sale. Thank him for doing business with me and ride off with my horses. I'll have them strung together or I can drive them back, herd them to my Livery, and business done. Simple as that."

"Either way, Skeeter, whatever makes you comfortable. I am just trying to help you the best way I know how."

"Let me think on it for a while. I have something I need to tell you," said Skeeter. "Truth is, I just found out the wife never stopped playing poker, the card playing business—you know, the one I mentioned."

"How do you know?" I asked.

"The neighbor, she been watching our children for Lizzy while she has been attending an evening ladies quilting bee. You know where a group of ladies all sit and make a quilt one after another. Well, Lizzy and Josie started running those poker games the same night every week as the quilting bee. I know where she keeps her money from her business. I checked when she was in the outhouse, and she has more money than she had made when she worked her game the time I was out of town for 2 weeks."

"Skeeter, don't ask her about what she is doing or the money you found. Just watch and keep an eye out. Act like everything is just business as usual. If your wife has an ulterior motive or a plan she is working, all that will come out eventually. It is not wise to speculate until you have some solid evidence of what she is up to. So far she has given you this money for the family business so why not give her some slack. There has been no crime committed and no wedding vows broken. Think about it, Skeeter, am I right?"

"I am a U.S. Marshall from Illinois with connections in St Louis. I was raised and trained by a Sheriff. I studied with the Pinkerton's while I stayed in St. Louis. This is what I would do. I have become very good at this profession. I am willing to stay here for the time being and work for you, and we will both be better because of it."

"We call it a cover, and you provide me that—a place to work from. What my real business is and why I do what I am doing is the undercover work you need to mention to no one.

Skeeter took his hand and made a motion like he was locking his mouth with a key in a lock. Then he smiled as he made the motion as if he threw the key over his shoulder.

"I have an idea—if I work for you as a hired hand or hired man, and you are possibly using the money you know she made, she might start to trust me, and I could see what I can uncover. What do we have to lose? We have some time to wait for the response to the two letters to travel to the K Bar B-Q Ranch and the bank and their responses to be mailed back."

"I might ride up to the K Bar B-Q Ranch and pick out the best horses. You will pay with the wire transfer released when I take possession of the horses. I will need another hand to help me bring the horses back—that is, if you don't trust Mr. Huffington to select your livestock and send two of his men to deliver them."

"I'll come over tonight and your wife can read the letters, and I will answer any questions and explain it to her. Tell her you can't or don't want to leave town. She will know why. Even if she don't say anything, she will, of course, suspect. Tell her you will pay me for my services from the profits of the sale of one of the horses. Tell her, I need a good horse because I have a lame horse. I am working for you to pay for a good horse and a pack mule to carry my gear when I leave. In all reality, she did finance the purchasing of these horses apart from how she came to raising this cash. What do you think?" I asked.

"I believe you, and it does sound like a good idea," said Skeeter. "The truth is your horse went lame and you're working for me to pay for a good horse. You prefer riding a good horse rather than a mule. You already own the mule we traded for."

Skeeter stuck out his hand. I shook the hand of this 6' 8" mountain of a man with the unlikely nickname of Skeeter. He said, "You're hired, Mr. Larry Dalton, Jr. But what about that man you're, aah, tailin?"

I said, "Skeeter, I have learned to never get in a hurry, especially in certain matters. When you hurry, you make mistakes; and mistakes can cost your life or the life of another. I will catch this man—I will, I always do."

Chapter Four

The afternoon moved along slowly as the summer heat settled on the town like a wet blanket of hot moist air that only Kansas could conjure. We were taking a long deserved break from the work of the day. We were both sitting in the Livery barn. Skeeter said, "We're done as far as work is concerned. We just need to stay here until 6 p.m. iffen any customers come. It's too hot to spend any more time tryin to bust our tails with work anyway. Let's just kick back—we will get the work done and take 'er easy the rest of the day."

"You're the boss, Skeeter," I said, wiping the sweat from my brow on the sleeve of my shirt. "I'll tell you the story of the first time I came out West. I sat in the saddle of a horse I purchased in Rolla, Missouri. The horse was old and plum tuckered out. He would lie down, and I couldn't get him to stand. I ended up with two mules I purchased from a livery stable in Hays, Kansas. They were a pair of mules from the Civil War, and they were almost a matched pair as far as their temperaments. They insisted on being together. I rode one and used the other as a pack mule."

"My Paw read me a letter from a cousin about two mules that were used in the Civil War with the very names I had chosen to call these two mules. I was told the names of the mules in the Civil War letter were Sprit and Tate. They were from a dirt poor farm somewhere in southern Virginia." The story was interrupted when a local man entered, and Skeeter was asked to go outside to see to some personal matter.

When he returned, I said, "Well, Skeeter, we have a few days until the letters are returned from the K-Bar B-Q Ranch and the Bank in Dodge City, Kansas. Do you understand how we are setting up the business for the purchase of the horses?"

"That would be ok, but first write down all we are doin with the Huffington ranch in Nebraska, and the bank, and the bank papers you mentioned." We walked into the tack room that doubled as a make-shift office. Skeeter found a piece of paper and said, "I have some schoolin. I went through the sixth grade back East. I know my letters and my sums, and I read and write well enough. But this new way of doing business is all new to me. I really trust you, boy, and I'm open to what you want to learn me."

I wrote down the information and then I took time to make it clear and simple for Skeeter.

The K Bar B-Q Ranch in North Plate, Nebraska territory, about 20 head of halter—broke riding horses at the low dollar price per head inquiring for the low bid price. The second letter was addressed to the First Bank at the Union-Pacific Trailhead, Dodge City, Kansas, concerning a "Letter of Credit" on deposit from a wire to the bank in North Platte, Nebraska, for a Mr. Peter Huffington, owner and proprietor of the Trading Post at the North Platte, Nebraska, Railway office, Union-Pacific, and sole owner of the K Bar B-Q Ranch. With this all in place, we will complete the sale of 20 horses to a Mr. Cletus Jonas Magnus, owner and operator of the business here in Kirwin, Kansas.

"I am sorry, boy. All that makes my head hurt. I have a better idea and a very simple idea," said Skeeter. "I have you stay here and run things, and I will go and buy the horses. I will pick the best mounts to my judgment. You run the livery here until I return. The worst thing that could happen while I am gone is my wife keep doin what she was doin before and make more money for me and the business. If she runs off to her relatives back East, either way I am the better for it."

I said, "That sounds just fine to me. You're the best man for the job in the first place."

"Well, that settles it. I'll get things together and leave in few days," said Skeeter. "Until then, I have a pot of coffee I brought from home, and we can warm it up. It's probably cold by now anyway. I have a half loaf of bread and some jelly we can eat iffen we have a need to COFFEE UP. This afternoon you can go get some of the donuts that the restaurant sold us. Here's two bits—more than enough to go get them, and we can eat um here."

"Now we got quite a bit of work to do. Let's get it done before we think about takin another break. You can tell me the rest of that story this evening at the house. I want you to meet the family. You will be working with my wife while I am gone to get those horses. Get up in the hayloft and get some hay. We need to clean out stalls and put down new bedding hay."

Almost 2 full hours had passed when Skeeter said, "We have fed all the stock and cleaned all we need to do to be ready for any business we might have. I have the coffee hot, let's eat some bread and jelly. You are in for a real treat—this bread and the berry jam is, well, DEE-WEECIOUS," said Skeeter. "That how my boy says the word 'delicious.' My wife and I both think he is caution. The word 'caution' is what my wife calls him. I, aah, don't really know what it means."

I interrupted and said, "Caution means concern, care, or warning."

"Thanks," said Skeeter.

The bread was as good as I have ever tasted and the jam was—well, it was just as good as the boy had said. Dee-weecious. The coffee was cowboy coffee grounds poured into a pot with water and brought to a boil and poured into a cup and cooled so as to allow you to drink it without scalding your mouth and tongue. This had happened to me on a few occasions, and I was on guard to never let that happen again.

Chapter Five

A tall man walked into the Livery asking about his horse and wanted Skeeter to get it saddled up so he could ride to another town. This man was introduced to me as Billy Wilson, Kerwin, Kansas, Town Sheriff.

I smiled at Skeeter and said, "I need to introduce myself to the Sheriff and inform him of who I am and about the man I was trailing. I presented the U.S. Federal Marshal's badge and told the Sheriff about the man I followed and lost just east of Kerwin. I told him who my father was and how I was assigned to this particular case. The Pinkerton's were very active in the case because it involved a train robbery in northern Missouri.

The Sheriff had heard of my father although he had never met him. His reputation had spread far from the Illinois county where I had grown up.

Sheriff Wilson told me the name of the Sheriff in the town he was riding to was Delbert "Del" Waldrip. The town was about 4 hours west of Kerwin. Sheriff Waldrip had arrested a man for property damage and drunk and disorderly conduct. He was being held for 30 days for this incident. The extended time for the crime was due to the extent of damage inflicted during the drunken brawl. The Sheriff has some wanted posters and believes the man may not be who he says he is.

He had bragged to a woman in a saloon before he was arrested that he had plenty of money buried in the ground back east from a train job. The possibility of using a false name and identity is the concern of Sheriff Del Waldrip of Hill Dale, Kansas.

Sheriff Billy Wilson was contacted this morning by a rider from Sheriff Waldrip of Hill Dale and asked if he had any additional wanted posters. I told Sheriff Wilson I had a wanted poster with a description of the man involved in the train robbery. I also had a separate drawing from a picture taken of the man a few years before. It was a family portrait but the man in question was right there in the middle back row. I had borrowed this picture from a relative of the man. A Pinkerton sketch artist had made a very good duplicate. How I acquired the picture is another story.

I was invited by the Sheriff to ride along as he went to Hill Dale, Kansas. I started to ask Skeeter if leaving was okay. He raised his hand and said, "You be about your business, boy. You come back, and we will tend to what we discussed."

I was riding the mare at the time I was briefly seen by the man. Now I was riding the mule I had most recently purchased from Skeeter. I borrowed a hat from the Sheriff. I left the coat I had been wearing for the last week in the tack room of the livery along with my saddlebags, bedroll, and accouterments.

I had never met the man I was pursuing, but I had seen him. I was sure he had never been in Illinois—not where I had lived and spent time growing up. A few days ago this man had seen me but it was from a distance that would keep him from identifying me as a U.S. Marshall. The incident happened 5 days ago. I was riding up over a hill and was surprised when my suspect was standing about 200 yards ahead in a small clearing by a grove of trees. I just reined around and rode back over the hill. When I checked a few minutes later, the man had skedaddled.

I was not sure if it was the man I was looking for on the poster. I was just following a tip from a man in a town that he had seen a man fitting the drawing of the suspect on a blaze faced, brown horse, white stocking on the right front foot. I was told the man had moved through that town and was long gone. It's better to use the drawing looking for your kinfolk rather than flashing around a wanted poster. This keeps an edge with the element of surprise. It also keeps down any suspicion. That's just me—that's how I think.

Skeeter moved the mount from one of the stalls and placed a beautiful Mexican saddle on its back. What a beautiful saddle. I could see a name carved on the large saddle horn but thought better of it than to be so rude to ask of the name. Sheriff Wilson said a man came through and traded the saddle and his horse to Skeeter for another mount and riding saddle. Sheriff Wilson had wanted to purchase the saddle from Skeeter. He was only allowed to use the saddle and flatly told by Skeeter the Mexican saddle was not for sale.

Skeeter suggested we use the rest of the bread and jam and make up as many sandwiches as we could and eat them on the way to our destination. This is what I did, slicing the bread thinner than usual, so we both had a few in a white bag Skeeter supplied and I tied to my saddle horn. The mule made a good mount, and I was pleased with my Jenny. That's right, I decided the first mule anyone owns might as well be called Jenny.

Chapter Six

The 5-hour ride started about 3 p.m. The arrival time in the town of Hill Dale should be about 8:30 p.m. The Sheriff mentioned that was good as we needed to arrive under cover of darkness.

Billy Wilson was a rather quiet man and was a far better listener than most men I had known. He had a way of asking a simple question that seemed to desire an answer. The time spent in travel was quiet at first. Then after some thought I told Sheriff Billy Wilson about my first trip out West, after the question, "Well Mister U.S. Marshall, where are you from and what brought you out West in the first place?" asked Billy. That was the start of a one-sided conversation that took up the majority of the time spent in the saddle moving west from one sparrow fart town to another on the Kansas plains.

I started by saying: "I am the son of a town Sheriff. I was raised by him and a mother who was a half-blooded indigenous Native American. My mother had numerous relatives who all delighted in teaching the young half-breed everything her people could teach a young brave every summer. In the fall I was in the white man's school. My mother took sick and died when I was 15. I have many memories of her, and I cherish every one. I had attended all the school grades and decided I needed to travel out West and seek all that the experience would afford. I eventually saved and earned enough money to pay for the trip West. I was 17 years old with every desire to seek every adventure that I could live to tell about."

"I traveled down to St. Louis and then south across Missouri to Kansas and on west to see what I might discover and experience. The stories of my first adventure out West are truly a story in itself. The time spent changed my life, and I value every experience I lived and would not change one thing."

"That was over ten years ago now. I have since returned to my Illinois home and went on to study in a school in St. Louis. I returned to work in my hometown with my father who was and is a Sheriff of a town in southern Illinois. I had spent time and studied with the Pinkerton school in Chicago, Illinois. I traveled to upper New York State and spent 2 years in training in Washington, D.C. I was appointed a U.S. Marshall, and that is my current job. I work out of the Pinkerton office in Chicago, Illinois."

"Well, back to the story. The horse I had purchased in St. Louis had thrown a shoe and was very spooky from the get go. This horse would shy away from almost anything. I was startled and taken by surprise more that a few times by the horse's erratic behavior. I decided I needed to stop and have the shoe replaced—better yet, sell the mount and get another."

"The closest town was Fort Hays, Kansas. I needed a horse, but the blacksmith sold me two mules. He told me the two mules were the best selection for life in the western frontier. I would need a second packhorse—in this case a mule. I acted like I had only enough money to meet the price with some $5 and offered to work for the remainder of the purchase price he was asking for the one mule. Well, I paid more than $5. When I was riding out, the mule I was riding started braying something awful."

"The mule stopped and would not move. That's when this second mule started and made such a ruckus in the corral. I finally asked the Smithy if the mules were a pair and were used together in pulling a team for some local farmer or company. I thought and finally determined after a convincing by the blacksmith that I couldn't buy one without the other."

"I started acting like someone who had been taken advantage of by a dishonest blacksmith. I was accusing him of doing this dishonest sales trick. I told him I was going to the sheriff and file a complaint with him and have a local or the Circuit Judge hear my case in local court. I would stay in town until the Circuit Judge came to hear my case. I would be granted both mules and pay half of the price I was being asked to shell out today. I then continued to threaten to go to the U.S. Army at Fort Hays. I would file a complaint with the military against the blacksmith, and because

I was the child of a sheriff, I would have a more favorable case to argue before a military judge."

"The blacksmith raised both hands and said, 'Please, please—listen to me, son. I have not done anything to you that I haven't done to those who passed this way before you. If you are offended, I offer my sincerest apology.' Walking back and forth wringing his hands together looking troubled, he finally said, 'Now you just keep your britches on, boy. Don't get your under drawers in a bunch.'"

"The blacksmith apologized and said he had not intended to do any such thing. I ended up with both mules, and the man insisted I allow him to buy me a meal at a local café. While I was eating, the blacksmith talked with me asking what I intended to do as I went out west. I was eventually convinced I needed a pack rig for the second mule. I must get supplies and stock up for the unforeseeable demands of the country to the west from the Smithy's friend, the storekeeper of the local General Store. The blacksmith insisted on taking me to the store and introducing me personally to the storekeeper. I had no idea he had actually planned this rouge in the first place just to sell both of the mules."

"The blacksmith paid for my meal and then took me to the storekeeper. The storekeeper sold me the amount of the total money I told the blacksmith I had after the purchase of the two mules. My poor attempt to conceal the true amount of money I was carrying was revealed by the blacksmith to the local storekeeper. The storekeeper sold me enough supplies to pack the back of the second mule—all of which I would surely need for my journey. I was convinced I needed large canvas saddlebags for the mule I was riding. Both filled with numerous items until they too were bulging."

"The two thought they saw a sucker coming. I was that sucker who you might say was hoodwinked by them both. What did P.T. Barnum say, 'We have a sucker born every minute.' I left Hays, Kansas, with two mules and a small general supply store loaded on the backs of the two mules."

"I took almost an hour the first and second mornings to tie down all the supplies on the pack mule. I spent the next 2 days moving west on the open plains. I had not seen anyone. I was constantly on the lookout for anything that looked suspicious. I was trying to find a campsite that was in a ravine or near a grove of trees. The water was very scarce. I had well packed bottles of various liquids. I was supplied with a bevy of dried beef jerky and plenty of tin cans of fruit and vegetables. I had traveled for 5 days, and mid morning on the sixth day I met a young Indian boy on the prairie. His horse had stumbled in a prairie dog hole, and the horse was in need of being put down. The boy was tired, dehydrated, and very weak and hungry. The dark bruise on his forehead could have clouded his judgment."

"I took care of the horse and did the only humane thing I could do to put it out of it's misery with the revolver my father had insisted I bring along for the protection of my life. By the suggestion of the storekeeper, 'You can never have enough ammunition for the revolver. What if you're found under attack by hostiles or a robbery attempted from Evil White Men. Why, just because it did occasionally happen.'"

"I placed the young boy on my mule. I walked and led the two mules some distance to a grove of trees by a stream and made camp. I fixed food and coffee for the boy. The skin was broken in the bruise on his forehead, and dried blood was matted in his hair. I helped him clean up. He was not acting, in my estimation, well enough to move, so we just stayed by the trees and the small stream. The water was clear, and I used it to cook and clean the pans when I had finished. I believed the boy needed this time to recover from the fall he had taken from his horse."

"I made a special tea to bring health and healing. I had learned about the tea from a widow in my hometown. I had the recipe written out on a large piece of paper. I was not surprised I had all the necessary ingredients needed to make it. I gave some to the boy and I took some myself. We both had liberal amounts each day, and the boy started to recover a little each day."

I have included this recipe below for you to try at your own risk—a treatment for what might ail you. Keep the tea in a cool dry place after making it. Why? Well, that's just what the widow lady said.

FRESHLY BREW GREEN TEA STRONG 1/4 TO 1/2 CUP

GARLIC THREE SECTIONS CUT UP INTO SMALL PIECES WITH THREE TABLESPOONS OLIVE OIL IN LARGE PAN.

SAUTE TOGETHER I MINUTE. ADD GREEN TEA 1/2 CUP.

ADD PURE CLOVER HONEY FIVE LARGE TABLESPOONS FULL.

ADD VINEGAR ONE TABLESPOON.

ADD CAYENNE RED PEPPER 1/2 TEASPOONFUL.

ADD 1/4 TEASPOON ASAFETIDA (OPTIONAL).

HEAT ALL TOGETHER IN PAN, BUT NOT TO BOILING FOR 5 MINUTES ON LOW FLAME.

STRAIN THROUGH A CLOTH INTO A GLASS JAR. LET COOL. REFRIGERATE OR STORE IN COOL DRY PLACE.

TAKE ONE TEASPOONFUL IN A.M. AND P.M. FOR BEST RESULTS.

THIS RECIPE AMOUNT WILL MAKE A 1-WEEK SUPPLY FOR ONE PERSON.

"We both used the time to learn signs and teach each other key words to communicate. We became good friends. We spent time together for the first 4 weeks after the original incident. We moved west as I had originally intended on traveling. I eventually learned the boy was from the Ogallala area—a Lakota Sioux tribe from what appeared to me to be in the far north. I told him of my mother and her people called 'Chockia'—direct descendants of the mound builders of southern Illinois. There are 200 counties in Illinois, many with the names of the Indians who lived in the area before the white man. I was soon referred to by Little Elk by the word 'Breed'—half white and half Indian. This was not new to me, for I have had this label all my life. I had a leather bound book with many blank pages. I used this book to make an English-Sioux and a Sioux-English list of words written out phonetically as close to the sound of the Sioux words as possible."

"I had so much in supplies and household goods, it seemed I was able to sell something to almost everyone we came across. I eventually sold almost every item I purchased for far more than I had paid for it. I had an inventory list that I insisted upon prior to leaving the General Store. The gold and silver coins and other things we needed was common barter as we met others who were traveling west. Some were moving east, but they were fewer than those who were making the trip west. I had almost double the amount of money I had paid for the supplies and the mules in the first place."

"We met some as we traveling on the open plains that were almost destitute and low on supplies. I gave food and supplies to these hungry people and asked nothing for it in return. I had an abundance of supplies. As I now look back on that first trip, I was truly a real green horn. What is a green horn? I really don't know where the term came from in the first place. I think it's an inexperienced new comer with no savvy. Savvy means knowledge, ability, know-how, savoir-faire, sense, and or confidence. Now we both know what 'savvy' means. I had a lack of savvy. That reminds me—I had ointment, suave, and medicine. I even found whiskey in small glass bottles wrapped in colored cloth near the bottom of one of the canvas saddlebags late in the trip."

"I can't say for sure, but it wouldn't surprise me if the storekeeper split some of his profit with the blacksmith. Although I have no evidence such a thing took place, I just know I was truly thankful I was able to sell most of the items I did not use. I had found some extra things I didn't recall ordering or on the inventory list like horehound candy by the dozens in little white bags. That hard brown candy was a tasty treat."

"I was taught or given a recipe by the storekeeper to make Pemmican. It's simple. Use white flour, ginger, cinnamon, pure cane sugar (optional), and water made into biscuits and baked in a cast iron skillet or a cast iron Dutch oven sitting in the hot coals of an open fire. The final product is similar to cinnamon flavored biscuits. They don't raise much and are somewhat solid—but with coffee, they are quite tasty. You might even say they taste good. The key word here is 'might.' I say, try some Pemmican and make up your own mind."

"I think the Good Lord was watching out for me. Some of the people on the trail were probably praying for what I was able to sell them. I gave away some of what I had for no charge to those who were in need and were unable to pay or said they were broke. I kept good records for what I paid and asked for a profit added to the price of each item I sold. I was impressed at the profit I made for the resale of all I had. What the two men had meant for payback or whatever their intention, God made all this happen for the good for me and a lot of other people."

"We both made a decision early on because of the way some of the whites were acting toward Little Elk, he being full blood Lakota (I as a half-breed knew too well how the white could act). Little Elk needed to keep his hair up under his hat and dress in my clothes to look as much like a white man as possible. This seemed to come natural for him."

"We both kept going west toward the mountains and finally stopped at the south fork of the Platte River—what was then called Auraria along the east side of the south fork of the Platte River. We visited the settlement of Littleton and a flour mill also along the South Platte in Colorado. We spent time with some miners, and they taught us how to pan for gold in the Cherry Creek. We both got really good at panning and were able to trade the gold dust we panned for real cash money. There were men who would come and weigh out the gold dust and pay you right at the edge of the Cherry Creek. We both thought this might not be the best price we could get. So we went to the inner part of the settlement of Auraria—eventually called Denver City. We met a man we both felt was a good man and could be trusted to buy our gold dust. We spent the summer panning, and we both had quite a stash of gold and silver coins as payment for our efforts."

Chapter Seven

"In the early fall we decided to go and visit Little Elk's people. We would pan for one more week and then make our way north. I had sold all I had left on the pack mule to the people all along the river. I had more money than personal items and the pack mule seemed to be smiling as the load was lightened on his back. Little Elk suggested we take some of the money and buy what we needed for the time we would travel north. We should also buy many things we could trade to his people. His people would not use coins, but we could trade for things they made and we could later sell to the white man. Little Elk told me what were the best and most needed things by his people."

"We again used the second mule to pack the things we purchased from the trading post on the south fork of the Platte River called the South Platte. The two large canvas saddlebags were again stuffed with supplies. Within a few days, we were packed and ready to travel north. Little Elk led the way, for he was going home, and he assured me he knew the way. There was some of the most beautiful country I had ever seen."

"We had traded for a horse Little Elk was now riding. We were met by what I would consider to be outriders or a security patrol when we first came near the large tribal encampment of cooking fires and tepees. I didn't know what he actually told the outriders, but they were not riding up all smiles until he started yelling something to the braves as he called them. The hostile faces quickly turned to smiles, and we were escorted into the village. Two of the most fearsome looking braves of the group rode ahead. When we were near the camp, the tribal chiefs and Little Elk's parents met us."

"I was officially invited into the tribe, so I decided to stay and live with the Indian tribe of Little Elk. Black Wind, as I found out he was also called, was the son of one of the families of the chief. Black Wind was the son of the chief's brother—that made him a nephew of the chief. I later learned Black Wind's people and family were one of the fiercest people on the northern prairie. They were very thankful for me saving Black Wind's life. He had gotten separated from a hunting party. He must have become disoriented, and he and his horse had moved far south and ended up where I eventually found him."

"I had the leather bound book and made notes of things I learned. I had used the book to make notes of the Sioux words that were needed to talk and understand Little Elk. I had English-Sioux and Sioux-English as I said before. Little Elk, as I called him, had traveled and traded with many of the other tribes—the Sioux, Cherokee, Ute, and Arapaho people."

"We met and made friends with many from the other tribes of the plains Indians. I learned so much of the verbal and oral tradition of these people. I recorded what I had heard in the leather bound book."

Chapter Eight

"I had so much to learn, and I spent almost 2 years with Black Wind's people. I have never been the same, and I will never forget what I learned of these people and their way of life. Much of what the white men say and record about these prairie people is wrong—how they live and their respect for the land, animals, and so much more. I learned and have so many skills and abilities no white men could even conceive. I recorded all I observed in one of the journals I had purchased from the Fort Hays storekeeper. The second spring after I had arrived, Black Wind came to me with an idea. The two of us decided to build a trading post along the South Platte in what is now northern Colorado."

"The idea Dark Wind had was we could speak both with the Indian sign language and the English the white man was speaking. That is exactly what we did. It was not new to either of us for we had done this kind of work twice before. We did this very successfully for 4 years. We were eventually convinced to sell out to a wealthy man from back East who was very persistent in presenting offers to buy the trading post. He finally said he was going to offer us an amount we couldn't refuse. He was right, and we took the generous offer."

"The payment for the trading post was divided and split between the two of us. It was all in gold and silver coins and was delivered in a black steel chest. We each took what we needed—a very small amount just to live for a few months. Black Wind, as he was called due to the cold night he was born, convinced me we needed to bury the coins and wait until a future time when we would decide to come and remove them and start another business. The chest was buried by a large tree in the dark of night on a hill overlooking the Platte River. Only the two of us know the exact location. I have yet to go back and check on the black steel chest."

"We had heard of the gold in the hills west of Auraria. This story was told to us for the 4 years we were operating the trading post. We were now both riding the mustang ponies of the Sioux. We ate the two mules the first winter I lived with the Sioux. We rode to the south and visited again the area called Auraria. So much had changed—more people had flooded into the area. I thought we needed to dress more like the whites. We purchased shirts, pants, and boots. Although we didn't start out wearing the boots, as the leather moccasins were far more comfortable. I told Black Wind he needed to have an English name. He said he would think on it."

"We are brothers; the white families have the same last name like a tribal name. I will be called Dalton. For we will be of the same white tribe or family as you would call us. I will be of the Dalton family, and my first name is Richard or Rich Dalton. I heard a man called this name when we were living by the trading post in Auraria, when we were panning for the gold. This was before we went north to stay with my people. His name was Richard or Rich Marlowe. He said he was a cook or actually, a master chef. He came out West to start an elegant restaurant. He was going to name it 'Marlowe's.' He decided on Auraria—or Denver, Colorado, as it is now called—to become the location of his restaurant. He would make his fortune in a lifetime of serving good food at good prices out here in a city at the gateway to the Rockies, eventually called the biggest cow town in the west."

Marlowe's—Downtown, 511 16th St., Denver, CO, 303-595-0471—for reservations

The Buckhorn Exchange, Denver's oldest, 1000 Osage, Denver, CO, 303-534-9505

Morton's Steak House,1710 Wynkoop St., Denver, CO, 303-825-3353—for reservations

"I remember that man, his name, and his story," I said.
"Dark Wind said, 'I will be called Richard "Rich" Dalton.'"

"'Your middle name is the last name of your mother—it is Smith—that is a way the whites name their sons.'"

"'I will be called, Richard Smith Dalton, I am Richard Smith Dalton, I am called 'Rich' my nickname, by my friends,' said Black Wind or Little Elk, or Dark Wind, as I will always call him.'"

"'My long black hair—it is the only thing that will make the whites think I am an Indian. I will have it cut and I will keep it short, no longer hid up under my hat. I will be a white man. In my heart I will always be a Lakota Sioux brave.'"

"I took his hand and pulled him close and hugged him. 'White brothers hug each other when they meet and it is a way to showing love for your family. I was made a brave of your tribe when I lived with your people. I am a member of the Chockia tribe even being a half-breed. I will always be a Lakota Sioux brave. We are warriors, we are blood brothers, and we are part of the tribe of the people.' I released him from the hug and said, 'Mr. Richard 'Rich' Smith Dalton, I am glad to meet you. I am Laurence 'Larry' Smith Dalton.'"

"He smiled and said, 'We will always be Black Wind and Deer Hunter.' That is the name I had been given by his people. I had used my ability to hunt and kill deer when the tribe needed fresh meat. I was just a good hunter, and I could find and shoot game. My father had taught me to fish and hunt in Illinois."

"We then went up to Black Hawk, Colorado, and made an unusual contact. We met two cousins, Jon and Frank Dalton, who were relatives from Lamar, Missouri. I introduced Richard and said 'This is my brother, your cousin.'"

We were just entering the town of Hill Dale, Kansas, when Sheriff Billy Wilson said, "You will need to tell me the rest of that story on another trip. We need to meet the Sheriff at his home. You stay in the shadows and keep out of sight if you want to make the plan you mentioned to me earlier work. I think it is a really good idea. You will need to explain the details of the plan to Sheriff Waldrip." We made our way through the town using back streets and an alley when finally Billy said, "We're here. You stay out here with the horses. I'll go in and talk to Del. We will need to put the horses in the barn out back."

Chapter Nine

I outlined the plan I had told to Sheriff Wilson in more detail to Sheriff Waldrip. Possibly this is the man who had committed the train robbery, believed to be Franklin "Frank" Beesley of southern Missouri. We would say nothing about the original crime. I would be supposedly arrested for disturbing the peace or a similar charge and placed in the cell next to this man. I have a visitor who would slip in a bottle of whisky. I would act as if I were not planning on sharing with the other man in jail—he being a stranger and all. I would, of course, eventually share my liquor. This man had often had a problem with a loose tongue when Mr. Barley Corn made his presence known. I was sure I could gain information or any secrets this man was so willing to share with a strange woman he had met and bragged about his hidden cash from a train robbery back east.

This would be easier after he was feeling his liquor. I would see if he was as talkative as he had been on prior occasions. Perhaps I can get some information to connect to the man I am looking for.

The local sheriff had what he said "was a better idea." He had the town printer print up a bogus wanted poster of a name he knew was safe and could never be identified by this or any other man. The printer made up a poster with the name of the sheriff's half brother who had lived and died in southern New Mexico. The charge was bank robbery. I was arrested, and told I was being held until I would be taken to the county in which I was charged. I would remain in this jail until the sheriff from New Mexico arrived. I was placed in the adjacent cell, but after 3 days I had no indication I would learn anything from the man.

I started yelling and asked the sheriff for a bath. I was at first denied one. I yelled the more and said, "It is a capital crime to allow a prisoner to smell any worse, and I am in need of a bath."

During my time out of the cell I told the local Sheriff "I have nothing. This man is being tight lipped." My original plan "A" was now the second and backup plan "B." I initiated the second plan as I came back into the cell with a bottle of whiskey hidden under my coat. I told my cell neighbor I found it in the bathhouse. Surely someone was enjoying a drink with their bath and forgot and left the bottle. When I revealed it to my cell neighbor, he showed great interest. I was at first reluctant and very hesitant to share this secret bottle with him. "There's not enough for the two of us. This is one bottle of whiskey, and I need it all for myself."

I finally relented and shared the bottle. During the night, sometime long before I saw the dawn of the following morning, to my delight, he revealed the location of a map to where the money was buried. The map was hidden in the right heel of the train robber's boot. I was able to talk very softly; and as I talked, my drinking buddy passed out leaning up against my cell bars. I removed the front part of the heel—with great effort, I might add.

The only paper I had was a letter in my coat pocket I had started to write and not finished. I had a nubbin of a pencil folded inside the letter. Using the paper torn from the unfinished letter, I had made a drawing of the original map down to every detail. I was about to replace the original map in to the heel of his boot when I decided I needed the original map. I then changed some markings on the duplicate and placed it back in the heel of the boot. I was actually able to doze off and slept for a time before the Sheriff arrived with morning coffee. I nodded and smiled. When my cell neighbor was just rousing awake and had a sniff of the coffee aroma, he started yelling for some of his own. The Sheriff returned with a cup of coffee for my hung-over friend. The stage was set and the Sheriff's plan would now continue to be preformed perfectly.

My hung-over cell neighbor would hear as I was informed by the Sheriff that it was a case of mistaken identity concerning me being involved in the bank robbery in New Mexico. The charges for the drunk and disorderly conduct and destruction of property would need to be paid. However a local rancher desperately needed another hired hand and had paid my fine for the destruction of the private property. In exchange for payment of the fine, I would work to pay back the money for the charges and the damages at his ranch moving some cows east to a railhead in Kansas City.

I was free to go. The rancher was waiting outside to take me to his ranch. I tipped my hat and smiled in the direction of my hung-over cell neighbor and walked out the door. Billy Wilson was sitting on his horse holding my horse by his bridal straps.

I was gone, but not until I had written out a sworn statement concerning the confession of the details, planning, and some specific happenings done by Frank Beesley during the train robbery. The first statement by the saloon dance hall girl expressed more detail to the amount of the money that was taken and bragging of how the train robbery was pulled off. It was identical to what I stated in my deposition.

To the surprise of our prisoner, a week later, two men with U.S. Marshall badges (Pinkerton's) showed up and took him into custody. He was transported to Kansas City, Missouri, for trial and eventual incarceration in prison for the conviction of train robbery. For Frank Beesley, crime didn't pay.

The Pinkerton senior agent gave Sheriff Waldrip of Hill Dale a bank draft for a $1,000 reward from the Union-Pacific Railroad for information leading to the arrest and conviction of parties involved in the robbery.

The reward was split three ways between Sheriff Billy Wilson, Sheriff "Del" Waldrip, and an unnamed third party. The split was as follows: Sheriff Billy Wilson $330, U.S. Marshall L. Dalton $330, and Sheriff Delbert "Del" Waldrip $340. It seemed fair at the time for Del to get the extra $10.00. It was his jail, my plan, and he was a close friend with Billy Wilson, so it was his call. It gave us all more than a year's salary all at one time.

We used a special age-old medicine to get this bad man to talk and confess to the crime we all believed he had committed. It was just a friendly chit-chat in the middle of the night between drinking buddies. We invited Mr. Barley Corn—or should I say,

Mr. Rye Whiskey. How does that drinking song go? "Rye Whiskey, Rye Whiskey, Rye Whiskey I cry, if I don't get Rye Whiskey, I surely will die." Old Mr. Barley Corn has loosened the tongue of more than one man who was a slave to it.

I didn't divulge the map with the possible location of the buried train robbery money with either of the local Sheriffs. I felt that was not a part of any deal I had or hadn't made with anyone—the local law enforcement included. This information and the original map were given to the Pinkerton men who came to escort the prisoner back to the jurisdiction of the county where the charges were filed. I would allow the Pinkerton team to pursue and find any buried train robbery money. The map was good and led the Pinkerton men to the buried money. It was returned to the Wells Fargo Bank, and a reward was paid.

I was eventually personally rewarded and received a finder's fee—a small percentage of the money offered by Wells Fargo for information leading to the arrest and conviction. The money recovered was a total of $100,000 cash and coin. I was called into the Pinkerton offices at St. Louis, Missouri, where I was presented with a letter from the president of the BNSF Railroad, a certificate of accomplishment, and a check for $500.

I sent a telegram to the Sheriff's office in my hometown. I secretly informed my father in this two-sentence telegram that I was all right, I had completed the assignment, and it would be 2 months before I would anticipate arriving home. Two months would reveal I was sent the draft from Wells Fargo to the Sheriff's office the token amount for the recovery of the funds stolen in the train robbery. My father would have deposited the check or draft into my checking account at the local town bank.

I used the 2 months for some sightseeing as the BNSF had given me a free pass to ride where and when I wanted for one year. I planned all along and included a side trip for Skeeter. I went up and purchased a string of 11 horses from the K-Bar B-Q Ranch. That's all they had at the time. I paid a local man to assist me as I moved them south to the livery stable in Kirwin, Kansas. I then sold the horses to Skeeter for the price I paid marked on the bill of sale. I did charge for the man I hired to accompany me for delivery and a 10 percent charge for my time.

Skeeter said he could possibly double his money on the horses. They were all excellent mounts. Skeeter then insisted I take one of the eleven for myself. I had sold the mule I had called Jenny to a man at the K Bar B-Q Ranch. I had also purchased a mount for myself at the ranch. I told Skeeter, I already had a good horse. Why not give one of these horses to your wife.

I suggested he give the gentlest mare—as a gift from the two of us to his wife for raising the funds to buy the horses in the first place. I was there the morning when Cletus Magnus gave his wife Elizabeth Shepherd Magnus the beautiful mare and a saddle that was truly the saddle for a lady. Her name was painted on the back of the cantle and flowers were everywhere a flower could be painted on a riding saddle. Few men have ever really been kissed, and the kissing spectacle that day was a sight to behold. Elizabeth "Lizzy" kissed Skeeter three times on the mouth (or Cletus as she insisted on calling him). I shouldn't say anything about what I witnessed. It was truly "a sight to behold." On that day if on no other, Cletus was a man who had really, really been kissed. I am sure he was properly thanked by his wife at a later time when they were home. I still remember that I thought to myself at the time, "I wonder if Liz has a sister?"

I later asked Skeeter what had happened to the mare I traded for the mule.

He smiled and said, "I nursed her along, and she is now the fine carriage horse of Mr. Doc Brown. I have two more orders for a carriage and a good horse to pull them.

Skeeter said, "Come here, you." Then to my shocking surprise he grabbed me and hugged me lifting me off the ground and there I was hanging in mid air, feet dangling. He then said, "I don't know who you are. I have never seen you before, and I don't know your name. But you are the best friend I never had and never met." He finally lowered me to the ground and released me, still laughing.

I said, "Hey Skeeter, got some time to go coffee up? We can go to that café and have some donuts."

"No, I do not—and you ain't goin either," said Skeeter. "I need to tend to some horseflesh, and you are going to help me. Then we will go coffee up and have some, well, well we might splurge and have some pecan pie."

I then said, "Skeeter, I hear that pie is Dee-weecious."

"You remembered how my boy says delicious, and you couldn't have said it better. Now put on these leather gloves and follow me. We have some stock to tend to. Then and only then it will be cold ice cream, warm pecan pie, and hot coffee. As a matter of fact, my wife does have a sister. But you, wha yu say your name was? No matter, you ain't gonna meet her," said Skeeter, laughing and pointing his finger.

The End—Fin Finecemo

Part 3

Blood Brothers
"Life-Long Friends"

A co-authored work by
Laurence Dalton (Deer Hunter) and Richard Dalton
(Little Elk or Black Wind)

Introduction

This story is co-authored in the year 1925 by Larry Dalton and Rich Dalton. They are also called Dear Hunter and Little Elk (or Black Wind which is Rich's tribal name). They both insisted we place this story at the end of the book "Dalton Family Adventures."

In March of 1925, Larry Smith Dalton, Jr., (Deer Hunter) was 69 years old—after all, he was born February 26, 1855. His life-long friend was Richard Smith Dalton, Jr., aka Little Elk or Dark Wind (his tribal name) as his people called him. Dark Wind took the name of Larry's twin brother Richard Smith Dalton except he added the Jr. to keep the mail separate at the Post Office. Dark Wind was thought to be a year younger than Larry Dalton.

This is a work of fiction based on historical word of mouth and not of any real life experiences. As we all know, some stories expand and seem to see some elaborated and hypothetical form in the retelling.

Character profiles with background and general information

Laurence "Larry" Smith Dalton, Jr., was born February 26, 1855, the third born son of Town Marshall Laurence Crow Dalton, Sr., and mother Martha Louise Smith Dalton. Richard "Rich" Smith Dalton was the identical twin of Laurence. He was of slender build with an agile and quick ability to move as an indigenous man who spent years with the people of his father's mother. Laurence and Richard were one-fourth blood indigenous males. It is a custom to have as the middle name the last name of your mother's maiden name. That was a way many whites named their sons.

Little Elk, sometimes called Black Wind, a Native American youth, was 16 years old in the year 1872, and almost 5' 9." He was a Lakota Sioux warrior. Larry met Little Elk on the open range west of Hays, Kansas, in the now Colorado territory on his first trip West. Little Elk had been thrown from his horse and was semiconscious when Larry found him on the open prairie June 15, 1872. His date of birth was possibly in the year 1857.

Little Elk, Dark Wind, or Richard Smith Dalton, Jr., as he preferred to be called, later in his life graduated from the University of Chicago with a Masters Degree. He returned for advanced graduate study and received a PHD. He used the name Richard Smith Dalton, Jr., and the home address of Laurence Smith Dalton, Sr., as his family residence on his original application for entrance to the University.

He told Laurence, Jr., "The books and the reading of them is like a man looking through an open window into another world. Some paint vast pictures with their words that flow through my mind. The mathematical studies are a language of perfection unto itself. The more I learned, the more it all made sense to me. I just seem to know the final answer—it just comes in my mind like it was an internal harmonic melody, music flowing on the breezes of my mind. I see the final result of the mathematical equations, and the answers are obvious to me. It's like playing a musical instrument—it just becomes easy. And the answers, I just seem to know them. I spent hours with a school teacher in Springfield, Illinois, after Laurence told me to take time and learn how the whites think from their education."

He said, "I think I have a natural ability. I have heard of an ancestral prophet of my people say words, I will do this thing." The summer after Richard's graduation, 6 years of study, he was sent a letter and was offered a teaching position at the University of Chicago. Richard Smith Dalton, PHD, accepted the offer and became a full professor for the University. Richard told Larry "I enjoy teaching almost as much as I enjoy reading and learning."

No one except for the immediate Dalton family ever knew this man was a Native American Sioux warrior. His true identity at his request was never revealed to anyone in the white man's world. He said, "What good could it possibly serve? It is really no one's business who I am, and where I hail from, or my original lineage. My credentials, my achievements, stand for who I am and what I have done. I am a degreed professional, a full professor. I graduated with honors as Valedictorian of my class."

"I am given respect and admiration for who I am and what I have accomplished. If it were known I was Sioux, I would be called names, dishonored by men who cannot read or write, and maligned by men having no desire to pursue any endeavor to learn either. That is a sad epitaph for any country, especially 'the land of the free and the home of the brave.' In France, Spain, and the British Isles, I was treated with the utmost respect."

Richard Smith Dalton, Jr., (Dark Wind) was assumed to be none other than the maternal twin brother of Laurence Smith Dalton, whose father and grandfather were local Sheriffs—respectable lawmen. Richard said, "My people where I am known and have lived—the immediate family and descendents for decades in Illinois are Men of the Law. I have excelled in higher education and taught in the University. I have chosen to be 'A Man of Letters.'" What he said was true, how he said it, made it mean what it wasn't. No one apart from the immediate Dalton family was ever the wiser.

Richard often boasted, "One afternoon in a Pub in England, Larry and I sang 'I Am an English Man.'" I suppose they thought we were English for our accent was perfect. It is only speculation that in the next generation the youngest son of Richard Smith Dalton ran for the Senate and served multiple terms in office. I have heard it said one of the great grandsons of Richard Smith Dalton, Jr., was an elected official and served in the House of Representatives. This man could have possibly been instrumental in presenting the bill that was eventually ratified and voted into law in 1978, "The Freedom of Religion Act," assuring all Native American people to have the right to practice their native religion.

Just how much influence did a man named Richard Smith Dalton, Jr., have on the unfolding history of this country will never be fully known. He might have had a not so distant relative who ran for and was elected President of these United States of America. After all, was he not one of the original North American people? Richard loved to stand and sing: "This land is your land, this land is my land, from California to the New York island." Was this not truly his land?

Laurence "Deer Hunter" Dalton and Richard "Little Elk" or "Dark Wind" Dalton were said to have been seen in their latter years dancing around the fires of the people of the Black Hills of South Dakota. That is another story both men, with smiles on their faces, just don't seem to be telling.

All parts of these United States were open to their travel and exploration. They were said to have traveled to Mexico and Central and South America. They were known to have worked aboard ships in the Atlantic and Pacific Oceans, which led to destinations east as far as France, Spain, Ireland, and England. To the west, they spent an undetermined amount of time in Africa, Indonesia, China, and Japan to visit the lands and people they had only read about. Rich—ever the teacher—with his brother Larry who was the scribe, always writing observations in notebooks they kept as they recorded their adventures as they traveled.

Larry told his father, "You wouldn't believe what we have done in all the countries we have traveled, even if we told you."

Larry, Sr., would boldly say, "Try me, boys. I have a few tales I will share. You start, and I'll see if I can match you adventure for adventure." Those stories have been lost over the years as they were only passed down by oral tradition, never written, not printed in a book for anyone to read.

Chapter One

" **Y**ou told me a story. I will tell you one," said Black Wind. My father told me many things about my grandfather who was a mighty warrior. My grandfather was born in the spring of 1810 or so we suppose. When he was a young boy, he asked his mother how many winters ago he was born. His mother told him she would need to think back and count them and tell him how many had passed since he was born. Later that day, she gave him a carved piece of wood with twelve grooves or notches cut in it with a knife. His mother told him all she remembered of the year he was born and each year after.

That day my grandfather took a piece of hide from a buffalo that was about the width of three of his fingers and as long as his arm. He made 12 cuts across the buffalo hide and rolled it up and kept it in his teepee. He made another cut mark every winter for as long as he lived. He made a life belt for my father, and he showed it to me. I made one for myself. My father has the life belt that was made by my grandfather.

After I was born, my mother was holding me. My grandmother, on my mother's side, delivered me. My grandmother, my father's mother, came into the room and told my father that his father had heard me cry when I was born. A short time after he heard me cry for the first time, my grandmother said grandfather had been waiting for his son's son to be born. Grandmother asked my father if she could take me to grandfather so he could hold me and bless the son of his son. My father took me from my mother's arms. He walked with me wrapped in the blanket of the colors of the family and carried me into the room where my grandfather was waiting.

My grandfather held me, and he said many things. He sang for joy at my birth. He was told in a dream this child is a boy child—a special child. This is a child of hope with great promise for his people. This child will live a life of fulfillment. He will walk with more freedom. He will stand as a new generation. He will be a part of the white man's world. He will learn many of the white man's ways. He will sit with them in high places. He will travel the land to the East where the white man is strong and many live in houses of wood and stone. This child will travel to the great waters. He will learn of their wisdom. He will learn of their ways. Nothing will be held from him. He will be a man who listens to the white man's stories. They will call him friend. The writing of the wasichus will be taught to him. (Pronounced WA-CHE-SHOS. Translation: white man)

The day will come when all that has been lost and taken from our people will be restored. My son's son will see this time come. He will see this day. He will live to see all that will be restored. The white man will allow our people to live and worship as they did for years before the white man was ever seen in this land. Much more was said that day. I have seen many things come to pass as my grandfather told my father and my father told me.

My father told me many things. He was at Wounded Knee December 29, 1890. He was dancing with those who were there. They were singing and dancing the Ghost Dance. This dance was believed to make the white man leave and the buffalo return. The solders came and killed many of our people there that day.

He was there at the greasy grass, where the two rivers meet, to see where General Custer and all the men with him died on the hillside across from the river. That battle later was named Little Big Horn. This happened June 25, 1876.

He was not at Sand Creek with Chief Black Kettle, November 29, 1864. He was later told what happened there that day. I have been told many stories of his life. I have tried to remember them all. I have dreams and have seen my father doing the things he told me. I see the stories in my mind. I see them again as I tell them. It is like I am standing there, watching as these stories unfold. Sometimes I smell the fresh dug soil, taste the dust in my mouth, or feel the smoke in my eyes. I feel the emotions as I speak aloud the stories of my people.

Chapter Two

G randfather was younger than my grandmother. This is the story grandfather told of the first time he and grandmother were aware of each other. Grandmother would say, I still see him today with his legs bent at the knee. The boy crouched just inside the door flap of the teepee. Slowly he crawled out the door. First he extended one hand out to the hard ground at the base of the opening. Then the other hand out and pressed firmly on the ground. Then he moved the left leg and then the right until he was completely out and crouched down on his toes. Hand over hand he moved away from the door. His eyes were staring straight across toward the next teepee. A small pup was asleep in the sun. The boy moved ever so slowly.

When he was just a few feet away, he moved quickly forward and grabbed the sleeping pup, forcing his fingers into the soft sides of the pup. He raised it up and turned and ran for the river that was a good 50 yards away. Screaming and yelling, the boy ran.

Still screaming, he carried and half dragged the pup. He felt a strange sensation in both of his hands. The startled pup was now frantically moving all four of its legs in the air, squirming to be set free. The pup's frantic protests were heard from his whines, growls, and fearful whimpers. As he ran still holding the pup in both hands, it felt as if he had a strange sensation flowing from the pup into his hands. This sensation made it hard to hold onto the pup, and it seemed it might slip from his grasp.

Losing his footing and tumbling forward, he lost his grip on the sides of the pup's body. As the pup rolled on the ground and gained its freedom, the small legs were quickly put to use running for a safe place to hide which did not appear to be anywhere close. The pup ran for the nearest lodge and disappeared out of sight. The boy was laying in the dust staring in the direction the pup had disappeared.

A young girl was standing watching the boy. The boy did not see the girl. He was now sitting with his bottom on the hard ground, leaning back on his hands. Slowly he looked around—it seemed to him someone was near, quietly watching him. The boy moved and stopped by a teepee. Looking around more intensely now, the boy saw the young girl standing 50 feet away by a rack made for the drying of hides. She was watching him with a half smile on her face. "What will this crazy boy do?" she thought. The two looked at each other for a brief moment. Then the expression changed on the boy's face. With a yell and a high pitched war whoop, he was up and running straight for her.

She stood very still as the boy ran wildly in a straight line toward her. She then stepped to her left and swung her right arm as the boy passed, pushing him to the ground. She used his momentum to send him rolling in the dirt. He was startled and slightly disoriented for a moment. Then he was up again. This time he was moving slowly toward her with both arms outstretched with a slight bend at the elbows. He was not smiling, with an intense look in her direction, and with a sense of determination on his dirt smudged face.

Sweat slowly moved down his forehead, leaving streaks as it mixed with the dirt on his face. The boy took his sleeve and wiped the sweat from his face and eyes. This smeared the sweat down his face and across his cheeks. His cheeks were red from the heat and the exertion he has given this intense rampage played out in the mind of this young child.

Her first thought was to run toward the other lodges. Then she thought to herself, "The river is far better to rid myself of this menace." She planted her feet, leaned to her right, and took a step as if to run toward the lodges. She hesitated, waited as the boy took a step, then she turned and ran off toward the river. She slid to a stop at the river's edge. She is left with nowhere to go. She turned and waited. She now stood with arms outstretched, palms open, hands ready. The boy stopped, with a blank expression, with no plan or idea of what to do.

Then laughing playfully, he lunged forward causing them both to fall into the water. The two splashed and rolled around at the shallow water's edge. The water was only 12 to 18 inches deep along the bank. Both were laughing and giggling from the sheer excitement of the moment. The unexpected coldness of the water caused occasional deep breathing between the giggles.

As they struggled to stand, the boy found his hand under the girl's garment. He thrust his hand up higher and started to squeeze the soft flesh on the inside of her right leg. With eyes wide and a loud scream of protest, the girl grabbed the outstretched arm of the boy. As she grabbed his arm, she pulled it out and up away from her. The girl's free arm was placed on the river bottom, and she tried to lift herself out of the water. She pushed with her feet to stand, which slipped on the smooth rocks and stones of the muddy river bottom. With every attempt of pushing to try to stand, she thrust herself out into the deeper part of the river. As she fell back into the water of the river, she landed on her bottom causing the water to splash behind her.

The boy's wrist was tightly held in her hand. The boy was pulled forward struggling to keep his head above the water. The fast flowing current of the water filled her deer hide dress, and it started to float up the girl's body. Still holding onto the boy's wrist, she looked down and saw her exposed body in the water. The dress was gently moving up and bunched just below her chin. As she floated in the stream, she saw the fixed stare on the boy's face. He was looking, wide eyed, mouth open, his gaze fixed.

She realized she was floating in such a way that her legs, stomach, and upper chest are openly exposed to the boy's staring eyes. She realized she was still holding his wrist and outstretched arm. She released it by throwing it in an upward motion into the air. She placed both hands on the floating deer hide dress and tried to pull it down to cover her exposed body. This did not help as the deer hide was tightly bunched under her chin.

She quickly rolled over in the river, throwing her legs downstream. As she moved with the aid of the now helpful current, the water moved the wet dear hide dress slowly back to its original place. When ready, with the use of her hands and legs, she stood up in the slow flowing river water. She walked slowly straight to the shore.

She turned around and looked directly at the boy who was now standing and walking toward the shore. As he reached the water's edge, he moved slowly out of the water about 20 feet upstream from her. He stood looking directly at her. Without a word, she turned and walked up the bank of the river. She turned and looked directly at the boy with a stern look on her face. She then held her arm out, pointed her finger at the boy, and slowly shook her head from side to side. Then she moved her outstretched finger from side to side matching the movement of her head. With one final look of a tense stare, she turned around and walked toward the closest lodges. No looking back as she walked off. Slowly ever so subtly she allowed a slight change in her facial expression until she was smiling to herself. She thought, "I gave that boy a sight he will not soon forget."

Chapter Three

The boy walked slowly and thought as he walked, "I have seen my younger sisters with no clothes on as my mother cared for them. They didn't look as good as this girl. I will see her again; I will do things she will like." He didn't know what to do or say. He would ask his very own grandfather what to do. Grandfather would know.

Grandfather told the boy, "You can talk to the girl; but if you do her work, you will diminish yourself in her eyes. When time passes and you grow in years to be a warrior and you still feel this way for this one, I will tell our family; and we will go to her family and state your intentions. We will take gifts, and they will give gifts in return if they are pleased with our intentions."

"Now today, my son, you go and wait for the passing of time. Only then will you know your heart. Time and experience will pass. As you become a warrior, you can tell me at that time your intentions. Until then, you have much to learn in the ways of our people. Do not concern yourself with these matters. Now just grow strong and gain wisdom from the older men as they train you to become a man of the people, and someday you too will become a great warrior."

The girl would be working and doing the work of the camp when the boy would show up and ask if they could talk. Time passed, and the boy would talk to the girl while she worked. One day she asked, "Why do you come to talk to me? Most men will not do the work of the women or talk to them as they work."

The boy said, "At first, I just wanted to be near you and talk to you. My grandfather would see us talking and ask me what we talked about. I would tell him, and he would ask what have I learned from you as you do your work. I told him how you planned the work in your mind—you would think with your mind at night just before you would go to sleep. You would think out what you wanted or needed to do for the day before you started your work. You made your work easier as you thought of better ways, faster ways to do the work. Grandfather smiled when he said, 'Most people just do the work that must be done and nothing more.'"

"This is a special girl. She has a gift for herself and others," said grandfather. He taught me to hunt, and one day he asked, "What would the girl do?"

I said, "Grandfather, she would stop and close her eyes and see herself doing whatever she wanted or needed to do. She would take time to stop and think what she needed to have complete at the end of the work. She would first see it completed in her mind.

Grandfather said, "Close your eyes and see what needs to be done and what was not necessary. I will tell you how I have learned to hunt the deer, antelope, buffalo, and some small animals. You visualize in your mind what I say. Then you will tell me how you see yourself as you do the things I have taught you. Finally, you will go and hunt and do what you have learned. We practiced this way—first verbal instructions, then visualizing what I was taught, and finally doing what I had seen in my mind. I was taught to hunt and all the skills a young man would need to know and do to be a warrior of our people. "Someday you will be a great warrior," said grandfather.

One day when I was standing and talking with the young woman as she was doing her work, I said to her, "I have found you are a wise woman in the ways of our people. You think the work through before you start. You plan the work and how to do it faster and better. This is what I have learned from you. I believe I will be a mighty warrior and great hunter. I will be far greater than the other warriors of our people because of what I have learned from you. You have taught me much."

Chapter Four

The beaver pond became a destination, a place to walk, for the two young people who wanted to spend time alone. The cool air blew across the smooth surface of the beaver pond. The water seemed to ripple more as the wind blew.

A small furry beaver was rubbing his right front paw across his right eye and down to the end of his nose. Then the same movement was repeated with the left front paw. After the time of grooming, the small animal stopped. Looking across the water he would move forward ever so smoothly and disappear under the water, and then his head would surface as he moved across the pond. The mate would remain and watch as if something or someone was there to be seen.

Then the beaver bent his body in what would appear to be in half and slip forward entering headfirst into the water. Disappearing under the surface, leaving only a slight ripple that moved in a circular shape, from the place the beaver disappeared under the surface of the water. After a slight moment of time, the beaver glided up to the surface of the pond. The nose and partial head were seen first. Then the back and only a small part of the tail could be seen. The beaver seemed to glide with head extended and body under the surface.

The water was held as it were, there in its temporary residence. This partially captive substance was forever moving over the top edge and many places in the sides of the beaver dam. The water that flowed over the top of the dam made a rushing sound. The splashing and rippled sounds were carried with it as it made its journey to the meadow below. It seemed the majority of the water was held in the large dam area. This was only in appearance. The dam could only hold the water that its capacity would allow. The rest would flow over the top edge and out the holes in the sides of the structure.

The fish from above were always swimming downstream and eventually into the crystal clear water of the dam. The beaver would dine continually on the fish that ventured there. To the far side and out from the edge of the beaver pond was a round, dome-shaped home, built and fashioned by the industrious river engineers. This round, dome-shaped place would be the house for the male, female, and eventually the young pups. They would most assuredly emerge in the spring—after the upcoming winter, which will make this pond freeze over. All will be covered with snow that covers the land, the trees, and all that lives and moves here in this part of the deep forest.

The pups were born every spring, the extended family of the beaver. They too would grow and work with the family and eventually move downstream and dam up the water—building a dam just like the dam and pond where they were born. They start another beaver dam and another family with the same type of beaver home on the far side of the pond closer to the mountain, out far enough from the water's edge to provide safety. The dam again holds back the water for a home and a place where fish can come and swim until they become a meal being the main course, and usually the only course for the beaver family. Finding a crawdad in the muddy edge of the pond would also provide a tasty meal.

This beaver pond was 2 miles from the village where my grandfather was born. The people moved every year to different places to spend the winter and the summer. The winter camp was usually in the same place, high and protected from the fierce winds that came with winter. Some areas were the best for water and large grassy areas for grazing the horses. Wild game was hunted for food. The buffalo were the main source of meat, and their hides were used for blankets. Their bones were broken and sharpened for tools. Nothing was wasted. Every part of the buffalo had a use.

The land near the river upstream from the beaver dams was the best place for a village in the summer. This area was also a special place for my grandfather. He would meet my grandmother, and they would spend time together at this area. The trees were plentiful along this wide canyon. The slow flowing stream would wind its way down to the large grass-covered meadow below.

In the fall of the year, this young man became a warrior. He asked his grandfather to go to the family of the young woman and take gifts and make his intentions known. This was the only woman my grandfather ever loved. She eventually cared for him in the very same way, and they lived their lives together until their hair was gray and eventually white. They loved and cared for each other all of their lives. Their children and grandchildren were blessed, and they found a young man or young woman who they could love as their parents had shown them by loving example. My grandfather and grandmother were together every day of their married lives unless a hunting party or a search for the buffalo took them away from each other—until they died together one winter very old and full of years.

Chapter Five

The time came that the white man was using many of our men as trackers, hunters, and scouts for the U.S. Army. The people knew that the white man's ways were not the ways of the prairie people. The times were changing, and our leaders knew we would change because of these white men. This intruder of the plains was everywhere, and they were many. More white people were coming every year, and they were taking the land, breaking up the prairie, and planting crops and raising cattle and horses.

The U.S. Army soldiers came to our summer camp, and it was decided some of our men would work for the Army. My grandfather and father were two of the first who left with the Army. Grandfather was named White Feather, and his son was called Little. Little would follow grandfather every day when he was small and do everything he saw his father do. He was given another name at birth—Red Fox. His father called him Little White Feather. As time passed with the years of working with the U.S. Calvary, the name Little was what my father was called.

That first year my father followed my grandfather to be a scout for the Army. That year my father met a white man whose name was Leonidus French. Little was young, but he too worked for the U.S. Army as a scout. Leonidus and my father became friends. Leonidus was told the story of my grandfather called White feather and my father always following him around when he was a very small child. So he was named a second name, "Little White Feather." The name some of the older people on the village called him occasionally was just "Little." So this name was one father used if he referred to himself and if he liked you. It was this name that he told Leonidus French was the name he called himself—Little White Feather. Little was the name Leonidus called him. The name Red Fox was a name some of the people still call him today.

This story is really about two men who met in the spring of the year 1875. They met and worked together for the U.S. Army. Leonidus French was 42 years old and was a Sergeant. He worked as a surveyor and was proficient as a mapmaker. This was his primary job for the Army. He was a veteran of the War Between the States, the Civil War. Leonidus worked as a private contractor with the Army for 2 years—1875 and 1976. His job was to teach and instruct military personnel how to use the compass and how to make maps and read them. Officers were taught the art of mapmaking. Every military man was supposed to know how to use a compass. When instruction was completed, Leonidus was enlisted as a trooper and served with the 7th Calvary. Leonidus told Little about his children and family and especially about his son, William Henry French, who said he wanted to work as a surveyor. The grandfather of Leonidus French was Peter B. French, Sr., who was a Methodist minister.

Chapter Six

The year 1876 was the year that General Armstrong Custer and the 7th Calvary moved north on the plains in search of hostile Indians who were off the reservation.

Leonidus French and Little White Feather had become the very best of friends. Little had shown up with the scout unannounced and unaware of the dangers Army life could offer. Little was small in physical stature. I believe he was about 43 years of age when he met Leonidus. Little was probably born in the year 1832.

Leonidus French was born December 29, 1833. He served in the U.S. Army Company G, 47th Mounted Infantry, during the Civil War. He was discharged March 29, 1865. He served with the U.S. Army 7th Calvary 1875 through 1878 as a private contractor surveyor and mapmaker. He died June 19, 1888. Leonidas married Nancy Catherine Epley French on September 13, 1859. She was born February 20, 1843, and died June 30, 1930. Leonidus and Nancy are both buried in the Grenola, Kansas, cemetery.

Little's father had three large white feathers sticking out of his hatband that were thought to be chicken feathers. Hence, General George Armstrong Custer called him White Feathers. Joe was another name he was called. The laziness of the soldiers was commonplace. Many would envy this exceptional Army Scout. The nickname that stuck was Joe. I know it was not his real name. White Feather was probably not his real name either.

"This story is of two people who formed a close friendship," said Leonidus. "Little, as he was called, is more of a signature than a real name. Little White Feather was the name Joe's son was called. I called him 'Little,' and he said it suited him just fine. I taught him to read and write the English language. I purchased two leather-bound journals when we were in one of the largest Army Posts. The Fort Laramie trading post was full of many such items. The two leather-bound journals were almost identical. One was for me and one for Little. I had an English worded journal with Sioux words as a learning text. Little had a Sioux Journal with English words as a learning text with pictures, drawings, and definitions. The journal was a great gift from me to Little. We made entries of words, definitions, and drawn pictures. Usually every evening and sometimes when we were on military maneuvers when we rested the horses in the afternoon, we would make entries in the journals."

The dream that Little had one night was about a fight or battle that would be coming soon. Little described the dream in great detail. He told me "You must not be there that day. I do not know the day, I will know soon." Nothing was said about the dream for about a month. Then one morning Little said, "I dreamed of the war again. Big bloody fight—many men die that day. It will be very soon." Without this friendship and this dream of warning, the life of Leonidas French would have reached a far earlier end. His life was spared because of a box of food rations that Little dropped on his right foot. "I am sorry, my friend, to have to do this. Soon you will understand," said Little.

This accident placed Leonidus in a wagon, miles from the upcoming battle. The closeness that developed between these two was of a true friendship. Although not relatives, you would clarify the relationship as deeply devoted between these two men. It was as the Bible describes a David and Jonathan relationship.

The realization that Little literally saved his life due to the seeming clumsy accident that caused Leonidas to stay with the supply wagon that day far enough away from the battle that surely would have placed him in harms way. Leonidus was usually riding with the 7th Calvary led by General Custer.

The early part of the day of June 25, 1876, found Little riding on the seat of a supply wagon. He was seated next to a young soldier. Leonidus was in the back of the wagon with his foot up to slow the swelling and possibly relieve the pain. They had stopped to rest and water the horses. They were under a large tree, and all thankful for the shade.

Little said, "Leonidus take your journal and write what I tell you." With pen in hand and an uncertain anticipation of what Little might say, he waited. "I see the Crow and Arikara scouts riding. They see many Sioux and Cheyenne in a large village. There are many, many more than I have ever seen together before. Sitting Bull, the Hunkpapa Sioux Chief, has had his people dancing the Sun Dance. He, Sitting Bull, had a dream—a vision—while the people danced. He was able to see and hear what the spirits tell him. He and his people will have a great victory. Many of the soldiers will die soon. He looks very old to me," said Little. I hear the names Crazy Horse, Lame White Man, and Gall. These are great men of our people. The greasy grass is the place next to the forks of the rivers known as the Little Bighorn."

The complete story was told, and Leonidus wrote it all down word for word in the leather-bound book. It was the description of what was taking place at that very time miles away. It was as if the man was a seer, a watcher, an eyewitness, a far off viewer watching all that was taking place. All this was happening to the north just a few miles away—a distance that would be far enough that not a shot or sound was heard. But all that happened was seen by a man with talents of seeing in the spirit, a reality that did happen and was now recorded in a leather-bound book.

It was unknown at the time, but later the young trooper who was driving the supply wagon remembered the detail and the specific things Little had said—the detailed story of the Battle at the Little Big Horn River with the greasy grass. Leonidus and Little said nothing but listened as the soldiers of the Seventh Calvary described the place of the battle until the wagon with the previously isolated trio now looked on the graphic hillside with General Custer and his men laying naked in the sun.

The story of the greasy grass is about a place few men have seen. The white man has only heard of this place as it was mentioned in history about a battle that was short, and the mighty Seventh Calvary were outnumbered this 26th day in June 1876. The Sioux word (or the Lakota word, as the Sioux people are now called) for "white man" is Wasichus. The word Wasichus is pronounced Wa-see-choo-s.

The greasy grass is an area along the Little Big Horn River where the grass has a texture of oil as it is pressed or trampled underfoot by the people as they walk on the grass along the stream or riverbank. The name of grease or greasy grass was the name the area had been named over time, as the people would frequent the river to remove the life giving water. The grass was matted and had the appearance of what we would consider to be greasy. After all these years, everyone now knows the story of what happened that day.

Leonidus and my father, Little White Feather, parted at the end of their time with the Army in the late fall of 1878. Leonidus rode east toward his home, family, and all that his future would hold. Little and his father rode west to their family and home. They wrote a final statement of farewell to each other in their leather-bound journals. Leonidus had drawn pictures of Little and his father as they served as Army scouts. Leonidus never again saw his friend and always referred to him as the best friend any man could ever have or want to have. "Not written in good sentence structure or proper English," said Leonidus, "but makes perfect sense to me and it suits me right down to the ground."

Chapter Seven

It was a cold November morning when William Henry French met a man and his wife walking on the sand hills of his Nebraska homestead in the fall of 1911. William Henry soon determined this man and his woman were an Indian and his squaw. They are cold, and the woman was with child. Both were facing starvation and death from exposure to the severe cold. William Henry shared his home on the plains. His home was the wagon that brought him to this place, now setting on the ground—the wheels removed, with the back of the wagon in the dug-out hillside that gave protection from the wind for man and beast. Adobe bricks were piled high on the front three sides of the wagon. Without a doubt, William was saving the life of this man, woman, and baby.

During the first few hours together with limited vocabulary and an attempt to communicate, William Henry removed the leather-bound journal from his personal items. He went to the section with the Sioux-English and English-Sioux list of words. The look on the faces of the two now warm and fed guests was an open and profound stare. The man then slowly removed an identical leather-bound journal and opened to the same glossary section.

They both soon discovered the similarity of the two leather-bound books that were from their ancestors. Little and Leonidus were two men from different peoples and cultures who met on the frontier and become the very best of friends. The books had found a way to come together and share again all that Little and Leonidus wrote so many years before. The books followed a path that crossed time and the Great Plains to come together again in another time, another place. The three travelers stayed with William Henry through the winter until the spring of 1912.

William Henry, the son of Leonidus, had saved three lives directly related to his friend Little. This was triple pay back in return for the time Little saved the life of Leonidus from the slaughter of the 7th Calvary, June 26, 1876, at Little Big Horn.

William Henry and now this grandson of Little White Feather were reading the leather-bound books their ancestors had written—the last entries by Leonidus and Little were in the year of their final departure in1878.

New entries were made by William Henry adding the story of lives saved—extending across time and to the next generations in the Nebraska sand hills in the cold and blowing winter of 1911/1912. William Henry recorded the continuing story in both journals—recorded in English in his father's journal and in the journal now carried by a third generation descendent of Little White Feather.

Chapter Eight

As the winter slowly retreated from the Nebraska sand hills that spring, Little's grandson ventured out to hunt and brought back an antelope which was butchered and provided food for the group.

The new addition of the baby brought the group to four. The baby had been delivered with the assistance of frontier doctor William Henry French. William had only been a part of a delivery one time before when a mid-wife begged his reluctant assistance while he lived in Supply, Oklahoma.

During the long cold days of winter, William Henry read aloud from another book—the black cover had only the two words "Holy Bible." It started in Genesis with the story of God creating the earth, the creation story of God creating man and woman, and the fall of man resulting in the need for redemption. He read of the promise and prophecy from the Old Testament in Isaiah and the very city the messiah would be born recorded in the New Testament Gospels. He proceeded with New Testament studies from the four Gospels about Jesus Christ's life, death, and resurrection. They continued with a study in Romans of how man can understand the purpose of God for man and the descendants of Little who could choose to make a life changing decision. In Romans 10:9, 10, and 13, "Call upon the Name of the Lord."

William Henry prayed with the man and the woman, and they both received Jesus as their Lord and Savior. William Henry gave them his Bible. Both made the decision and prayed with full understanding of what they were doing. This was also recorded in both leather-bound journals. William Henry wrote the date and the names of the man and his wife, or squaw as he called her, in the front of the Bible that was given to them. What a legacy for Little and Leonidus, years after both had slipped into eternity. Their descendants are still giving and saving the physical life and building the spiritual life as well. I now have the journal Leonidus passed to his son, William Henry.

Closing thoughts and some clarification

This concludes what I have written concerning the life and times of Little White Feather and myself Leonidus French. The Sioux youth saved my life, the life of his friend. We all owe a great debt of gratitude to all of the Native American people for what they have experienced living in this land for centuries—now peacefully sharing with us in spite of the mentality of the George Armstrong Custer generation.

The previous and the present generations, for lack of a better word, the now—generation Americans—the people of this land. How else would you explain it? "Another generation grew up and knew not what the earlier generation practiced." Simply put, the masses, the majority of the people of this country seem to be unable to comprehend anything but to destroy and deplete our natural resources. The belief and practice of caretaker or protector of the precious resources of the land had passed with the prior generations.

The first peoples' respect for the land had made them caretakers who lived for centuries in harmony in the mountains, on the front range, and on the vast great plains. It was home for centuries to the prairie people from coast to coast from border to border. I respect and admire the Native Americans. I have met, come to know, and deeply love some of them. I know them, I call them my friend in every sense of the word, and I pray for their souls. Signed, **Leonidus French, U.S. Army Calvary, Retired. September 10th 1876. Also Signed and dated by William Henry French, April 12th 1912, Sand Hills of Nebraska.**

This is "The End" of the co-authored story "Blood Brothers Life-Long Friends," a work by Laurence Smith Dalton or Deer Hunter and Richard Smith Dalton, Jr., or Black Wind—both fictional characters as are all characters in this book. This is a work of historical fiction compiled from verbal and oral tradition. Any reference to historical people or historical places and or locations or any similarity to anyone living or dead is purely coincidental.

Letter from Frank Dalton
to Larry Dalton

The letter below is a letter Frank Dalton wrote to his cousin Larry Dalton, Jr., in southern Illinois in the winter of 1925. This letter might have been an inspiration to write about some of the adventures these men experienced in their lives.

Dear Cousin Larry Smith Dalton, Jr.,

It is my heartfelt desire you are in good health and this letter finds you feeling fit and your life prosperous. Everyone here is doing well. I am doing some travel, as it is one of the things these days I seem to gain great pleasure from.

I was with you and your young companion when you were two young men of adventure in Black Hawk and Central City, Colorado. I was so pleased to see you on that morning, not expecting you to be so close when it was apparent you came from afar.

The young man who was traveling with you was introduced as Richard "Rich" Dalton. You later took us into your confidence on the day we were parting company. You informed Jon and me that he was a pure blood Sioux warrior from the Dakotas who was named Little Elk, also called Dark Wind or Black Wind. I have never told a living soul of this man or his real or true identity.

So much happened after we parted company that I felt a needed to write it all down. My children and grandchildren are constantly asking Jon Dalton and his wife Susan to write the stories of that time in our lives and have them published in a book. It was really quite an adventure now that I think back. At the time, it was just what we needed to do to make a small fortune that has served both of us well.

I purchased a new fangled invention; well, it's new for me. I have an Underwood Typewriter. It was originally invented in 1895. The one I have was made in the year 1901. I have decided to write the story of my life experiences. I could send you a carbon copy as they call it for you to read. I think it far better to send a book of the story when it is completed.

That is the proposition I am offering to you. Will you commit to do the same with your life and Mr. Richard Smith Dalton? Simply hand write out your story in a letter and send it to me. I will have it typed by the typewriter and send you a copy of your work.

I will take your story and have it published in a book. I will send some finished books with colored covers to you. We can have this done in Kansas City, Missouri. I have a printer who will do the printing. His company would take our typewritten stories and set the type and have them printed in a book for all to read.

What do you say, Mr. Laurence "Larry" Dalton? Let's make it unanimous and both get started.

Yours truly—Best regards,
Frank Dalton, my wife Rose Wallace Dalton,
and our four children frd/rwd

William Henry French—
a Brief Family History

This was taken from "The French Connection" with research and compiled by Norman Payne.

William Henry French was the son of Leonidus French. He was born April 21, 1862, in Wayne County, State of Missouri.

William Henry's great grandfather, (Leonidus' grandfather) was Peter B. French, Sr., born in 1762 and died in 1849. His father was also named Peter, and fought in the American Revolution. Little information is known of him. Peter met and married Rosanna Rule (Ruhl) who was born in 1773 and died in 1830 in the vicinity of Lancaster, Pennsylvania. The approximate year was 1793 when they moved to Botetourt County, Virginia, on the James River—in the vicinity of Springwood, Virginia, which was and still is considered a "Low Dutch" (German) community.

The name of Peter B. French first appears in Botetourt County Personal Property Records of Hugh Allen, on April 24, 1793. The name of George Rule, (Ruhl) Sr., (father-in-law of Peter B. French, Sr.) appears in 1801. Followed by John (Jack) French in 1803, William French in 1809, and Thomas French in 1812. George Rule, (Ruhl) Sr., died in Botetourt County, Virginia, on April 12, 1819. His will, Volume C, 393, probate September 1823, mentions his seven children, including Rosanna, wife of Peter B. French, Sr. The name Peter French last appears in Botetourt County records in September 1815. He sold out the last of his holdings there, after purchasing lands in Knox County, Tennessee. Court records show he recorded the deeds of 204 ½ acres of land on Stock Creek (Dec. 20, 1816, W-D-1, Page 353).

Peter French's first commitment, after the land purchase, was to the Lord.

A log meeting house, 20 feet by 20 feet, was designated as a place to hold religious services. It stood on what is now Martin Pike at Tipton Station Road. Whether the structure was standing at the time of the purchase, or later erected by the French's is unknown. However, Rosanna Rule French immediately gave it the name of "Salem" and the road became Salem Valley Road—later renamed Tipton Station Road. Rosanna Rule French, died in 1830, and was the first person to be buried in the New Salem Cemetery. Peter B. French, Sr., married his second wife, Mary Rule, about 1840. She was a cousin of Rosanna Rule. Peter B. French, Sr., was a Methodist preacher, and preached in the meeting house on Salem Valley Road. Someone, possibly a relative, could still have a copy of his sermon notes or his Bible. Oh, yes. He did have a son named Peter B. French, Jr. This man was the father of Leonidus French, the grandfather of William Henry French and great grandfather of Howard Henry French.

Peter B. French, Jr., and an uncle possibly named James French were to have been circuit riding preachers, church planters in the state of Tennessee. This would truly be another story. One quite worth telling, I would think.

This is only the "**The End**" if we choose it to be.